TEARS IN A GLASS EYE

BOOKS BY KEVIN ROBERTS:

Short Fiction

FLASH HARRY AND THE DAUGHTERS OF DIVINE LIGHT

PICKING THE MORNING COLOUR

Poetry

CARIBOO FISHING NOTES

WEST COUNTRY

DEEPLINE

S'NEY'MOS

STONEFISH

NANOOSE BAY SUITE

ABOVE MARSHALL LAKE

TEARS IN A GLASS EYE

KEVIN ROBERTS

Douglas & McIntyre
Vancouver/Toronto

89 90 91 92 93 5 4 3 2 1

Douglas & McIntyre
1615 Venables Street
Vancouver, British Columbia V5L 2H1

Canadian Cataloguing in Publication Data

Roberts, Kevin, 1940–
Tears in a glass eye

ISBN 0-88894-640-6

I. Title.
PS8585.023T4 1989 C813'.54 C89-091054-5
PR9199.3.R62T4 1989

Cover illustration by Mark Schofield
Cover and series design by Barbara Hodgson
Typeset by The Typeworks
Printed and bound in Canada by D. W. Friesen & Sons Ltd.

For Maria, Anthony and Jonathan

ACKNOWLEDGEMENTS

The author wishes to thank the Canada Council for its support. He also expresses his gratitude to A.P., C.B.M., D.E., R.S. and D.B.

1

I KNOW THEY'LL BE COMING for me one day. There'll be a strange phone call, or the car that'll crawl down the potholed driveway, back up, and disappear, or the visitor or tourist who'll walk along the tide line when the sea has retreated, maybe with a camera or binoculars, who'll turn, casually, from observing the blue heron immobile in the tide pool to focus on this cabin half-hidden behind a stand of firs. Yeah, I've been lucky so far. Maybe I'm paranoid. Nothing will happen. Nobody's interested any more. No one over here even knows Australia was involved. Now it's a half-hour historical TV show like all the others, not even a popular one. A burning village, smashed buildings, a few statistics, a helicopter overhead, a shot of soldiers single file in jungle that could be anywhere, a close-up of demonstrators' mouths shouting outside an anonymous building.

It's hard to believe I was there, or to believe the luck that brought me here to this island. I take the Australian penny from my pocket. The 1915 is worn smooth. So is the kangaroo. It has a tiny hole on top for the cord that Wacker used to hang it from his neck. Wacker got it from his father who wore it through Tobruk. Wack's grandfather had it new in Gallipoli. It's got heritage, that penny. I spin it high and catch it. Tails never fails. Wacker's faith. I don't look, but put it back in my pocket. I'm sure it's tails. It's my talisman. My luck. The last thing Wacker did was to jerk it from his neck to put in my hand before I took off. I suppose it's a matter of luck. But I'm pretty sure you can't get away with what I did. You can't break their rules. They are inexorable, the slow churning of information until suddenly there's a blip, a coloured spot, an aberration in the system, the spinning computer tapes stop, back up, and then there's the question, the puzzle, the name, the number unaccounted for, and then the slow turgid electronic search for the answer. Maybe I'm wrong—they've written me off. Maybe they're not even interested any more, but I doubt it.

And right now I am happy, here in hiding, two years of peace, here on this island I came upon by a fluke, by a mere glance at a tourist brochure, on the run in San Francisco airport, all gloss and false blue seas and happy tourist families sunning themselves on the beach. This place is not really like that at all. Right now, the snow is a shining crystalline cover right up to the sea which looks like dark sluggish oil. The clouds hang in grey soft puffs, opening now and then for a distant vista of gaunt mountains, softened in this season by the smooth blanket of snow. North and south of me there's a spine of mountains like a drowned dinosaur, and huddled in little inlets like this one, clusters of houses and cabins, all cut out from the rich forests that cling in a thick blanket of dark green to the clefts and ridges and slopes and cliffs. And the trees. Such wonderful wood. The fir's cream white strength, the cedar's rich red marbled whorls, are soft to the touch, pungent to smell, even after years of grey weathering. This cabin, for example, framed in fir, rough cedar inside. I reach out now to touch the soft cedar planking on the wall, push gently with my thumbnail and leave a half-crescent imprint, a mark forever. Cedar's the same lustrous wood the Indians use to carve into their mythical creatures: raven, bear, salmon; and the mystical hovering Thunderbird, Sinekwa, wings up like Christ, beating; blessing yet ominous all at the same time.

The one mask I have, hanging above the bookcase on the planked wall, is savage and beautiful. I picked it up for twenty dollars from Joe Bob one night in the pub. The lips are pulled back and down, in laughter or derision or pain or hatred or all of these. The hooked nose looks like an eagle or a bird of prey. And the eyes in the black stained wood are empty slits, just blank unseeing holes. Two hanks of unruly hair, Joe Bob's, I reckon, hang from either side. It reminds me of a face I've seen many times. Desperate, empty.

The bookcase is full. Shakespeare, Conrad, Hemingway,

Lawrence, old university English textbooks. Yvonne brought them to the cabin for me. She wants me to grow, to understand. Sometimes I'm not sure exactly what, but I'm reading them all, slowly, picking up on all the distilled understanding they offer. Not that I was so dumb before. I reckon I was smart enough. While I'd read a few books, none of them meant a hell of a lot or made much difference to someone who was crutching sheep or lumping wheat. I just wasn't ready to find out then, thought I knew it all, had it made. But now I want to understand. I love the way the writers control what you see, how you feel. They can see into the guts of things, give you a different dekko every time. I'm amazed. I copy, or try to imitate their styles, the way their eyes create through the prose. Again that's Yvonne's influence.

After we'd got through a few preliminaries we ended up one night in bed; I thought it was great. But she sat up afterwards and said, O'Donnell, I love your body. You look a bit like Warren Beatty. But (and here she touched my forehead) I'd like to know you have a mind.

I was pretty pissed off.

Whaddaya mean? I growled, I can think.

Okay, she said, What books have you read lately? Well, that bloody threw me. But I'm quick off the lip.

Bugger reading them, I said, I'm writing the bastards! Now that got her interest! So I showed her some of the notes I'd made so far. About myself and where I was and how I got here. Not the ugly stuff mind you, but bits and pieces. She sat there and read them in bed. I was in awe at how fragile her back looked, the line of tiny bones, the frail shoulders. A maze of tiny blue veins crisscrossing just under her skin. Her breasts have the same blue lines. Sometimes I'm almost afraid to touch her. She seems so delicate. Anyhow, she read for a while, and then turned to me. This is quite sensitive, Jack, she said, it shows real insight. Maybe you do have some talent, she said thoughtfully.

That's how the whole damn thing began. Now we're at it all the time. No. I don't mean just screwing. Discussing books, or rather arguing about them. She says I've got a primitive male view. Maybe I have.

2

IT'S STINKING HOT. The land stinks. We stink. I can smell Harris, just up ahead. He stinks like stale piss. We're slogging down this dusty road, rice paddies on either side. We're supposed to check out a bridge ahead. Someone heard some shots there last night. Probably bullshit. I'm fantasizing about cold Foster's and tanned Ellen Montgomery, Miss Woodville—sixteen and sweet as a melon, on the beach at Boomers. I saw her often at school, adored her from a distance. I've got her white bikini shrinking bit by bit in my mind until the top of a pink nipple appears. It's hot, and sweat burns into my eyes. It's either raining like a bastard here or dry as a lizard's turd. The lieutenant is back at the rear being carried by Horsfield and Martin. Poor fuck can't hack it. Shouldn't be here. He's sick with fever. But he insisted. He dropped to his knees half a mile back. His eyes went up into his head. We carry him in turns.

Wacker's got two guys wide out ahead slogging through the rice paddies, two guys ahead in the ditches. This area's been pretty clear of VC for a while. But that means fuck all. They're in and out like a rat up a drainpipe. Right now my bush hat feels like it weighs two hundred pounds. This is a stupid exercise. Maybe we'll find a few empty shells where some Yank went crazy for a minute and shot a water buffalo. That's common. Overhead there's that constant hollow boom of jets like ancient angry gods.

Wacker hand-signals me forward. There's the bridge shimmering in the heat. A dinky wooden affair over a little river. Thick jungle on either side across the wooden logs. There's something glinting there in the sun. Wacker signals us into a wide fan as we approach. He puts me on point; I don't like it. It's too quiet. There ought to be some kids playing nearby or some Nogs in the fields. I'm not going across the bridge. It's probably booby-trapped. I crouch and run for the edge of the river bank. Roll over put my head up quick and down again. There's a big black Mercedes with some flag on the mudguard. I roll over the bank quick and wade through the water turning constantly side to side. Up the bank. The limousine is parked by the undergrowth. I run and stop. Run and stop. Two bodies. Three. And a fourth over behind the Mercedes. What the fuck is a Mercedes doing here?

I check out the area. Nothing. Francis is weaving in from upstream, Little Sam's coming in downstream. The corpses lie face down, their hands tied to their heels. Long hair. I think they're women for a second. Civilians. Couple of hippies. The backs of their heads are blown off and black now with insects. A pair of granny glasses lies smashed at their feet. Assassination. No wire. No booby traps. I roll them over. Get a shock. Two of them are Americans. One has a long nose. The other two are Vietnamese. One of the Yanks, long nose, has a slight bulge around his waist. I pull out a slim money belt. Whole bunch of money. And some letters. Christ. I shove them in my pack quick. Think of taking the watches. Don't. Nothing in their pockets. Who are they? What the hell happened? I stand up and wave Wacker and the boys in. He sets up a perimeter. Comes and looks. Byzantine, he says and spits. It's his favourite word for the fucked-up world here. He signals Martin over and calls in on the radio. The lieutenant staggers up, sees the dead and bloodied heads, pukes, and falls to his knees. He's white and sweating. Nog fever, we call it. We sit and wait. Twenty minutes. A jet kabooms overhead. Half an hour. We eat. That's the army for you. Hurry up and wait. And then helicopters. Womp. Womp. Womp. Dust everywhere. Six of them. Marines jumping out. Yanks everywhere. Dozens of them. A colonel. A major. We must have found something pretty big. Four civilians. It's unusual.

One of them asks, This is how you found them . . .?

Yeah, says Wacker.

The colonel and a CIA guy confer. He has a big baby face.

Wears dark glasses, a white shirt and civilian trousers. Shoulder holster with a .45 Colt. Total spook gear.

Nothing touched? he asks us.

Nope, says Wacker.

They get on their radio. A lot of talking back and forth.

I know I'm in deep shit if I say a word. The colonel walks up.

Okay. Thanks corporal. You can return to your base.

We slog back. The lieutenant recovers enough to lead us through the gates. Makes him look good. Wacker spits in disgust.

Back in camp I discover ten thousand dollars U.S. in the belt. Some documents. Wacker reads them. Shakes his head. Burns them in the rubbish tin. I keep one for a souvenir.

Wacker reads it. Byzantine, Wacker says. Absolutely Byzantine. What are you talking about? I ask. But Wacker just laughs. I'm pissed off. He knows something but he won't tell me. He throws backs his freckled red-headed face and laughs into the dark Vietnamese sky. I grab the letter back. We bury the money and the letter in plastic quick smart under our bunks. It's the beginning of my nightmare.

3

IN THE NANAIMO PET SHOP the rows of green, blue and yellow budgerigars natter and gossip in rows on their perches. Above them in two cages are six cockatiels, dark grey backs, soft grey fronts, white flash on their wings, more mature than the budgies in their stance, their head plumes erect as hussars. And isolated in one cage, a young cockatiel nods as it sits on the single perch like an ancient sage, its colours not yet formed.

What about that one? I ask.

Well, it's a difficult bird, says the proprietor. Fights all the time. I can't put it in with the others. Bites, too. He holds up a forefinger with a Band-Aid. The young bird wakens suddenly. Fixes me with its small dark eyes. Yvonne has sent me here to buy a pet. I look at the cockatiel. It's an outsider, like me. Does it wink?

I'll take it, I say.

4

YVONNE PREDATES THE COCKATIEL by about nine months. I had arrived at Malaspina Inlet, on the run, you might say, from some gambling and warfare and hustling in Oceania, found this run-down cabin, with its vaulted cedar ceilings and its sleeping loft, and paid a year's rent in cash. I had begun to put down such notes as these in the perhaps misguided belief that writing the past might clarify it, or at least cut a path through its tangled overgrowth so that I could see whence I had come. All that turmoil, blood and chaos I felt must mean something, or at least have co-ordinates that could be mapped.

I was sitting at the kitchen table, a wonderfully textured affair of uneven planks of maple, alder and oak, all dowelled and uneven and cracked and hence fighting within itself to disintegrate. Sitting, I wrote a few notes before the unmistakable sound of a VW engine, that flat blat and cough, came echoing down the potholed driveway. A soft knock on the door. Again. I climbed quietly up into the sleeping loft. I hoped whoever it was would go away, but I hadn't locked the door and it opened. A voice—I've tried to describe it before—calling, Anyone home? Mr. Thompson? That's the old name on the letterbox. Yvonne's voice is somehow musical; it raises and lowers more than most people's. It has the timbre of a musical instrument with a low register that can surprisingly reach beyond expectation.

In she came. Slowly. It's so typical of her, I know her now, how she acts, not exactly nosy, or aggressive, but wondering, interested, concerned. The perfect social conscience. She touched the copper kettle on the stove. Hot. She blew on her fingers. Dark hair, auburn, I suppose, down to her shoulders, a touch curly or unruly, stray strands here and there. She wore a dark green tweed jacket, almost like a man's Harris tweed, a blue skirt, dark brown boots and a leather bag slung over her left shoulder. I remember thinking with a bit of shock how she reminded me, the way she stood, of a smaller version of Wacker. Or, maybe I was just wanting to see him. I've talked it over with her a bit, now, the possibility of latent homosexuality. She finds it hilarious. Anyhow I called, Hello, from the loft.

Oh, she starts, turning. Her upturned face is round, the high cheekbones almost Slavic, the nose long and straight, the complexion not quite ruddy but pink cheeked. She smiles. It's a broad grin. One I'm becoming used to. A self-defence; she uses it everywhere, all the time. I think of reading about smiling in humans being the equivalent psychologically of dogs and other animals baring their teeth. Maybe that's what we really do when we grin. But it's her eyes that grab me. They are the sea. Green and dark blue, I can never be certain. I should know. But everything changes. It's the light I suppose, or the peculiar way I seem to see her, a blue, perhaps not changing, but variable within specific parameters.

I didn't mean to barge in, she says pointlessly, hunching her shoulders and holding her hands before her a tiny bit in apology.

I'm down the stairs now, find she's about five foot eight, has on a white blouse with significant bulges. I look at her eyes again. What can I do for you? I ask, a little uncertain of myself, as she makes eye contact quite seriously and holds it. Something I don't like to do, normally. A whiff of perfume comes to me.

I'm collecting names for a petition—she fumbles in her bag and pulls out a folder—to prevent the nuclear subs from coming up here from the U.S. She pauses, seeks my eyes again, but I look out over the bay, at the grey tendrils of rain swathing the horizon.

I'm sorry, I shrug my shoulder, I'm just . . . not interested.

Oh. She gives a little, staccato laugh. Now she's crestfallen. She stuffs the petition back in her bag, looks up, prepared to leave. I've given her no entrances, no beginnings.

Dramatically, it was at this point that I made my great mistake. If I had kept looking out the bay window, she would have walked. But instead, within my pocket I spun Wacker's coin and caught it, felt on my thumb the faint but too familiar tail, body and head of the roo. Tails never fails. Did I cheat? Another whiff of perfume. I don't know. It's how they leg-trap animals, the sex gland sprinkled on the jaws of the trap. I probably wanted to be caught. Yes. Honestly, I wanted to see that auburn hair spread out on my sheets upstairs. I wanted to feel the softness of those bulges in her blouse, discover the inner secrets of that skirt, the legs, the thighs. And so on. It had been a long time. And again I felt guilty, rude, antisocial, crass, arrogant, male. I turned and said, awkwardly but apparently with enough mustered sincerity to convince her, I'm just making a cup of tea. Would you . . . I didn't finish. Damn it, I thought, if I'd offered her a Scotch she would have suspected a seduction. But tea! So innocuous. So socially proper. You idiot. You've done it now. She turned. Again, the smile, broad and wide, and the eyes of the sea searching for mine, for that contact, that special connection. God knows what she was looking for, or had already seen, or intuitively knew. I'm six foot, still skinny, have a foxy kind of face, spiky dark hair, a big hooked nose, big ears and a long neck. That's irrelevant. Women see something else. I could see her doing it. It was frightening. I dropped Wacker's coin into the bottom of my pocket.

Yes, she said. That would be lovely. Have you lived in this place very long?

It was the beginning of a never-ending inquisition. I turned to the kettle. The flames underneath it were intense, like a violent red flower.

5

FOR THE FIRST TWO DAYS the cockatiel sat slumped on its perch in the brand-new cage I also bought from the Nanaimo Pet Shop. Whenever I approached, it hissed and snapped with its beak. The bird seemed stunned. It stared out the window at the wintry bay beyond the icy garden and ate nothing.

I became worried and put fruit and cuttlefish on the pegs on the bars of the cage. The bird ignored them. You must eat something, I said with concern, but the cockatiel turned its head slowly and fixed me with its black eyes in a look of deep and utter contempt.

Perhaps it's homesick, says Yvonne that afternoon on her triweekly reconnaissance of my domestic status.

For what, I ask, Ayers Rock?

I don't know. Something, answers Yvonne. Boy, it's hot in here.

Sorry, I say. I keep the heat turned up for the bird.

What about this bird, says Yvonne, coyly reaching down to grasp the sides of her angora sweater. She pulls it off over her head. Through the silk blouse her nipples are soft brown stains. My reaction. Simple, saurian, sexual.

Yvonne, come here, I say and pull her down on the couch.

Jesus, O'Donnell, she laughs, you're insatiable.

As we begin making love, the cockatiel bursts into a frenzy of chattering and jumping. The cage rings and sways and the seeds splatter. Yvonne is her usual vigorous, demanding self.

Almost desperate.

Look, Yvonne gasps, it's eating. It's come alive!

I think it's a voyeur, I say. Come on. I'm alive, too!

6

WHEN DID I FIRST HEAR the bird speak? I'm not sure. The voice seemed to trickle into me slowly, at odd moments, a seep, like a pinprick in one of those abominable plastic bags of cheap Canadian wine. And with a similar effect.

The first time I remember hearing anything I thought I was dreaming.

'Od's blood, the voice muttered. In what manner of devilish springe is this woode cocke caught? Startled, I looked up from my desk and about me. No one. Except the cockatiel. Yvonne's forced company against my perceived loneliness sat upright on its perch. It stared impassively out the bay window. Was I hearing things? A vague echo of something Shakespearean, sixteenth century?

Is that Shakespeare, I asked, the great bard?

Shakespeare! squawked the cockatiel angrily, that phony boring long-winded, rhyme-churning prick of a poetaster! Stolen plots. Five acts of hyped iambics and pathetic puns? Racism, severed head, gloomy guts and wimpy princes. His only real character was a fat man! Don't give me any of those Elizabethans. Webster! Beaumont! Fletcher! Just simpletons! Blood on the floor and a whore at the door! Blood on the floor! Blood on the floor and a whore at the door!

The cockatiel shrieked, and in a rage flew at the bars of the cage, its beak snapping viciously. Shakespeare! The cockatiel defecated two yellow bursts. It was a form of aggressive literary criticism from the bird I would become accustomed to, finally.

7

MY GREAT JOY on this island is salmon fishing, or more correctly, trolling for spring salmon, also known as tyee salmon or in the Crazy States, ironically, for its overt Republican stance, as king salmon. Somehow the slow probing of the depths, the undulating investigation of the dark recesses of the deep pools out there in the bay, has the analogy of a search for truth; is a ritual of religious significance for me, an enactment of the primeval search, the quest for destiny. All of which explodes in that second when the twenty-pound silver muscle strikes at the herring and runs.

Fish? queries the cockatiel with a strange tilt to its beak as if some odour of decay had wafted by. Those near-reptilian fossils who never did have the brains to crawl out of the primeval ooze? Of what possible interest could they be to a person of intelligence?

The bird nods sadly. Of course, I have, *ipso facto,* answered my own question, it adds, but surely you can find a more sophisticated subject for your amateurish attempts at writing?

Yvonne's perspective presents yet another angle. Presented, pink fleshed and baked, the aluminum foil pulled back to reveal the moist ribbed delicacy, with scalloped potatoes, and a good Barossa Valley riesling with beads on its cold outside glass, she has every capacity to delight in its existence. But fishing. No. She gets cold, bored, impatient and seasick in that order within forty minutes. I think she hates fishing. At least she hates the killing end of it. I don't mind. I prefer the solitary endeavour for its reflective quietness, its constant dicing with the unseen far below.

In the winter, on this island, I literally have to fish between storms, in those hours between fronts which bring the vast rolling clouds and storms one after the other swirling in from the Pacific Ocean over the backbones of the mountains and which dump heavy loads of rain onto this long thin strip of shale and rock. In that space between fronts, the bay takes on a platinum smoothness, an unrippled millpond broken only by the swirl of seals, the harrying dives and thrusts of the sea gulls on the herring, or the occasional riffle of some tiny gust of wind, come and gone quickly in the stillness.

I keep an eleven-foot nine-inch Springbok, an aluminum boat, turned over beyond the sea's reach on two derelict logs. It takes a minute to pull it to the sea's edge, load the rods, oars and gear into the boat and row out to where I've learned the tide, far below, washes over sunken cliffs and dropoffs, tumbling the food to the springs, which by nature seem quite indolent, and can only be enticed into hitting at a lure or bait when it is worked so close to their strike zone, it virtually bangs them on the nose.

The cockatiel flies to my shoulder at this moment, reads what I'm writing, offers me instant criticism.

What pretentious shit your prose is, the cockatiel observes dispassionately. Look at the diction—that phrase—quite indolent. What's wrong with lazy? And back a bit. Solitary endeavour. Undulating investigation. My lad. Don't you realize how bourgeois your language has suddenly become? You're showing off your new-found abilities. Or trying to, and it sounds pathetic. Stick to the strong gutsy Anglo-Saxon words more suited to one of your class. You're a hit and shit writer, not a strike and defecate Parisian poncified prosodist.

Fuck off, I say, enraged at the bird's interference, I'm flexing my wings. Trying to find out how to write like you learned to fly, I reckon.

Yes, I suppose that's a lot better, reflects the cockatiel. Imitation is the sincerest compliment. It flies back to read more Proust.

Fishing's the same bloody problem. The dream and the reality. Yvonne, squealing and crying, pulling her knees up and covering her face as I'm smacking away at a twenty-two pound spring I've played and netted, trying to whack the fucker on the head with a priest, eighteen inches of round hardwood, and the fish, not pooped out enough, banging about and out of the net and about the boat and Yvonne screaming, Let it go! Let it go! and me cursing, You fucker, stay still you rotten bastard, and belting away at it until the blood splatters and it finally shudders horribly and is dead. The silence then is clear, undiluted, except for Yvonne's sobbing at the savagery. That's more like fishing really is, I suppose. I don't know why Yvonne gets so upset about it. You've got to kill to eat. Any farm kid knows that.

But I prefer those great moments, rowing and resting, the rod tip nodding quicker then slower, rowing, and the rod tip pecking away, just about straight down to the ten-ounce banana weight and the five-foot leader with the herring, tied with a double hook, one through the cut plug, one through the back, bobbing and weaving like a cripple a hundred feet down in the dark, and the rod suddenly bending, bending right down. And you forced to wait, count to three until the herring is right in its mouth and then smack it, hit it, rear the rod straight up in the air and feel the solid weight of the salmon tight on your line, before it runs, the reel, a Penn, screaming, something like a high-pitched saw, as the fish runs, keeping the line firm as it turns, runs again, taking up the slack, the rod pumping and the salmon sometimes pulling the boat—keep the tension on, wind furiously—as the salmon runs back, and then the jump, the great silver head shaking and splashing and another pulsing burst under the sea and another, until the fish moves up to the surface, dark finned back, tries a dash or two and then turns over so its silver looks bronze bright. The big trick is to lead it head first over the net with your rod high in your right hand and the net, submerged, in your left, get it in and tangled up in the green cord, and pull the strange bright creature from the sea.

But, as in all Edens I suppose, there is the snake. This one is the occasional U.S. submarine surging black and silent in the strait. At times, I've been close enough to see a figure on the massive conning tower. They come up here to practise firing their torpedoes. Nowhere is safe, even this green paradise. Everywhere there is the hunter and the hunted. Even fishing for salmon.

I hadn't thought about salmon fishing as killing. I suppose it is. But it's not like hunting. I went once three months ago with a boyfriend of Yvonne's workmate. Yvonne wasn't keen on the idea, but I thought I'd see how I reacted to it. High into the rocky spine of mountains. The bloke, Fred, was crazy. Carried a .308 with one up the spout all the time. I had borrowed his old .303 and kept the loaded magazine in my jacket pocket. We wound up over logging roads and washouts to one of the high logged areas. Blasted down. Like a B-52 raid. A tangle of fallen logs. We walked along an ancient skidder trail in a valley. It was bitterly cold. Wind blew sleet in our faces. He was crouched over and walked tense and tight. I let him get well ahead but always in sight. He took three shots. I didn't fire. It reminded me of too much. I saw what probably was a buck up on a cliff about two hundred yards away. I walked slowly towards it. The deer didn't move. Seemed imperious up there. Sniffing the air for does, I guess. I got about a hundred yards away. It must have seen me. I could see the white patch on its chest, stubs of antler, two or three point, I suppose. I put the magazine in. Click. The buck didn't move. Pulled the bolt out. Click. In. Click. The bullet seated. Raised the sights. The buck stayed dead still. A damn little hole, a peep sight. Put it on the white chest. I could see the wind riffling its fur. Bang. Fred fired farther down the valley. The buck started and trotted away. I ejected the bullet, walked back to the truck. I don't think I could have shot it anyhow. It was a strange experience. Almost as if the buck were offered to me in some windswept solitary ritual. It's not that I couldn't kill any more. As Wacker always said, that was the savage lesson. You could kill. If necessary, anyone anywhere. That's what Kurtz knew out there in the Congo, I now realize. Took me a while to work it out. Yvonne says no, but I think Kurtz took complete control. Went over the edge out there. Like Vietnam. Like Wacker. Kurtz told the Russian, but he didn't understand. Neither did Marlowe, civilized wimp, liar, phony. Yvonne doesn't agree. She thinks Marlowe did the right thing. Stepped back. Lied for civilization. But Wacker drummed that into me. First principle. Survive. Fuck the rest. Wacker was right. Kurtz was right.

Fred turned up at the truck dragging a little buck like an oversize rabbit. I didn't help him gut it or skin it. I never went hunting again.

8

IS THIS BIRD MALE OR FEMALE?

What need of sex does a cockatiel have? Alone in a cage with no stimulation. Yet this bird called me to it last night. Sat on my shoulder and whispered of how it had to get laid. A simple matter. Dry black tongue chattering softly in my ear. Let me out. Where's the nearest tavern? Let me out. Where's Doll's Cathouse? Where's the brothel? Let me at the sluts.

I'm busy, I say, bugger off. You cretinous clod, spits the bird. It grabs the pen in its beak, twists it away from my fingers.

You're wasting your time writing. You should be enjoying the delights of the flesh while you can.

Pig's arse, I cry, piss off. I want to get this down.

It's pointless, screams the bird, besides you can't even get the colours of Yvonne's eyes right. They're aquamarine you dolt. And her hair is darker, more like burnt sienna. Can't you at least get the facts straight!

9

LATER THAT MONTH Wacker hears a word of a big *swy* game at some hotel in the Chinese district of Saigon. Biggest two-up game outside Aussie, they say. All the outfits are pooling their money and sending their best two-up experts. Americans, Kiwis, journos, Koreans, Chinese, the biggest players are expected, the stakes a minimum of a hundred dollars a throw. The lieutenant is only too happy to get rid of Wacker and me for two days. We dig up five grand of the money and wangle a ride into Saigon. There's this smell of cooking and shit and gasoline fumes. Scooters zooming by, mobs milling about, little kids flitting here and there, selling their older sisters. The street is full of Chinese, bargaining and shouting. Smoked eels and gutted chickens hang from the roofs of stalls. It's chaos again.

You can buy anything in Saigon. Cambodian marijuana cigarettes in a pack from the cigarette stalls, speed in a drugstore, a taxi girl for a packet of Tide, a pearl necklace for twenty dollars, a length of silk (the real stuff) for ten dollars. Everything is for sale in the noise and hubbub. There's talk you can get an AK47, a new one, for about thirty dollars U.S. It's crazy. Of course, there are three prices in Saigon, the highest for Yanks, Aussies next, and Vietnamese the lowest. It makes sense. We're rich by their standards. A Vietnamese soldier only makes twenty dollars a month and his general rips off half of that before the poor private ever sees it. So, everything's pretty cheap. A Bacardi and Coke for five cents. A bottle of beer a bit less. Bami Ba beer. Terrible muck. But we drink it even though it's guaranteed to give you the shits for a week. And a steam bath and a girl for two hours for about a dollar. But Saigon is also dangerous. There are all these Vietnamese cowboys, dressed in black, riding scooters. They should be in the army, but somehow they avoid it. Last month, one of them rode past sidesaddle, a passenger on a Honda motor scooter, and put six shots from a 9 mm revolver into a couple of Kiwi soldiers. There was a rumour that the New Zealanders had been plugging schoolgirls. We all knew they were off limits. Hell, you could tell them by their white *xo dy*, or white pajamas. Young kids. Beautiful but strictly untouchable. So I'm nervous all the time as we jostle and pick our way through the endless parade of people. In this carnival you see nothing but faces.

We find the hotel, finally.

We'll book in, says Wacker thoughtfully.

Why?

If the game's busted, no one'll look here. We can just duck upstairs to our room.

The room comes, or so it seems, complete with two Vietnamese girls, not very pretty, but enthusiastic. We don't even bother to remember their names. We bundle them out, and go downstairs to find the game. It's in an ancient ballroom out the back. There is fading gilt scrollwork and decaying plaster colonnades, four big fans moving slowly overhead. It's bizarre. The French, I suppose, had their colonial glory here once, officers and gentlemen and ladies waltzing about the crystal punch bowls, with bowing Vietnamese servants in tuxedos and white gloves.

Now it's a brawl. Dozens of sweating soldiers draining beer cans, shouting, standing in a circle watching the kip flip and the two coins fly; ten big blokes in civvies stand in the corners. Muscle and order. There are Yanks, Kiwis, Aussies, civilians and a whole bunch of Chinese. Chinese love to gamble. Big stakes. Five hundred dollars quite common. There's a little hush as the coins hit the ground and then the collective sigh and shout. Wacker eases his way to the front of the circle. I follow. As we planned, we wait for the rules of this game to come clear. It's different than other ones. Looks like they're taking doubles of any kind. Special bets on the side. Odds and evens and you can call the evens. A Chinese bloke squats next to us over a pile of U.S. dollars by his thonged feet. Must be three or four grand. We wait, as we planned, for a run of heads. Four to be exact. Then Wacker's flashing two grand and waving and shouting to get it covered for two tails. He gets two offers and slaps four grand down at his feet.

Tails never fails, his flushed and freckled face shouts in my ears over the hubbub. The kip flies. We win. We double up. Win again. The Chinese bloke is busted and curses us, waves his hand and melts back into the crowd.

No more, Wack, I yell in his ear.

Chow oy, he yells back, give me a break!

One more. Tails never fails, he grins, and waves a wad of dollars. Too many of this mob stop and watch. I don't like it. We've won too much too quick. They could get pissed off at our luck. But we get covered and there's a bit of a strange hush as the kip flies and the two coins roll and fall tails up. Wack grabs the money. Christ. We must have twenty-five or thirty thousand. We stuff it in our pockets and turn to leave. The mob turns to look at us for a second. Then someone calls, Come in Spinner! The coins fly, and the uproar begins again.

We emerge from the crowd to run into two of the burly house men. One has a baby beef face. Big bastard. Blond eyebrows. Blond fuzz. He looks familiar. The other looks Italian. Swarthy face.

Donation for the house? the biggest one asks.

Nearly forgot, says Wacker and hands him a fistful of Yank dollars. Probably a grand. We whip up to the room and count it—$22,473. Beaucoup bucks, smiles Wacker. It's more money than I've ever seen in my life. I duck down to buy beer from the hotel bar. Grab a bottle of champagne. The two Vietnamese girls see me and follow me back. What the hell. Wacker fingers the old Aussie penny around his neck.

The old man told me he won five hundred quid once on a boat back from Tobruk, Wacker reflects. Did him fuck all good though, on the Kokoda trail.

What about a drink, I cry, for rich bastards like us.

Two hours later we're so pissed we laugh our bloody heads off, looking out the window, as the MPs raid the game downstairs and cart off the two-up players in a bunch of army trucks. The two girls laugh at us in turn, naked, dancing, squirting champagne on each other.

I'm laughing and dripping with champagne as I look out the window again and see the two big blokes who hit us for the thousand-dollar donation, now wearing MP bands, and helping to throw the other poor uniformed sods into the trucks.

Jesus, Wack, look, I cry, it's those two blokes. They were bloody MPs all the time. It was a setup. Jesus.

Wack staggers forward for a peek.

Byzantine, he mumbles and falls back laughing onto the bed, his arms around both girls.

We wake up the next day sick and sorry. The girls have gone. Pinched about a hundred bucks. Fair enough. We hitch a ride back. Harris meets us at the gate. Some MPs have been in, turned over everybody's hooch. Ours is a mess. Bunks over, gear in a heap.

Nah. They found fuck all, says Harris. We had our dope in the latrines.

I start to worry, but they haven't seen where we buried our stash. Wacker grins. It's a huge joke to him. We bury the rest of our loot in plastic bags under our bunks.

Next day we're out on patrol.

10

KAFKA WOULD PISS HIMSELF laughing at my situation, observes the cockatiel over lunch, turning a fragment of rock melon with one delicate claw slowly before its beak. How long is this white shit out there going to last?

I don't know, I say, sometimes for weeks.

Christ on a crutch, cries the cockatiel, I don't mind snow on postcards, but how the hell can anything survive out there with a foot of that stuff blocking out the earth?

I want to go home! The bird begins to sing. Waltzing Matilda, Waltzing Matilda.

Jesus. This bird is a complete nationalist pain in the arse.

Australia. A melting pot just like the States. Pour all the immigrants in, melt 'em down into moulds and out they jump, bronzed Anzacs ready to get their guts eviscerated for you name the cause. Canada's different. You couldn't get a decent war going here if you tried. Nobody gives a stuff outside their own province. They're not stupid enough to wave flags just to get shot at. Just like a huge sponge, they absorb all the patriotic madness, think it over, and squeeze it out the other side in some bland shitty compromise that doesn't hurt anyone. It may not be heroic, but Jesus, it makes a lot more sense than what I've seen. Where I was, the truth was found to be lies, as Gracie Slick says. Logic and proportion disintegrated, the men on the chessboard—knights, bishops, kings—all stood up and told me where to go, into some vortex of an acid trip that was real, where the White Knight was talking backwards and the Red Queen was definitely off her head.

I turn over the record. Don't you want somebody to love, don't you need somebody to love, yeah, Gracie, I'd better find somebody to love.

11

WHY DON'T YOU ASK that gorgeous creature to live here? asks the cockatiel over breakfast.

Yvonne?

Yes. Ah, Yvonne. The cockatiel slurps over a slice of avocado. I miss her presence. About the table lie strewn bits of cereal and seed, fragments of raisins, apple, whole-wheat crackers. The bird's appetite is small but diverse, its demands for variety in food ever-increasing, its table manners nonexistent, and its arrogance growing in leaps and bounds.

We need a different social and emotional perspective, adds the cockatiel. Frankly, your conversation is pretty limited. And there's nothing like a female to brighten up one's life. The *je ne sais quoi* of *lares et penates*, the exquisite lace on the dull certainty of linen, the rainbow of femininity in a dull cloud-ridden day. The spice in the boring dish, the thread of gold in the grey cloth of existence. Ask her over. See what she says.

I'm trying to write, I say, but the cockatiel flies off and returns with my pen in its claw.

This, says the cockatiel, dropping the pen in my Weetabix bowl, is an instrument of death without love. Without love you will write nothing! *Niente! Nefas! Nada!* I can see it already. You're going nowhere.

Listen, I say, irked by this cockatiel's presumptions, I've tried it. Yvonne is a great girl, but she talks inanely and endlessly and interferes with my peace of mind. She puts everything away so I can't find it. She has me eating on time, sleeping on time, and living on time until I'm breathless with anxiety. I can't work with her around, and that makes both of us miserable. Anyhow, it's none of your business.

I rise from the table, pick up the plates.

Misogynist! spits the cockatiel and flies in a huff to its cage.

12

YVONNE IS GREAT at getting stuff out of me, after we've made love. We chat away. She can sift through all the bedroom chaff and come up with the grain or two of truth all the time. She talks a lot about her work, about books she's reading. Not much about herself. Often I'm just rambling, exchanging reminiscences, raving on about school or work or family, fragments of the past. She seems to gather it all together to form this collage, this connected picture I haven't seen of myself before. I still keep her a long way off. I haven't built a full picture of her. I keep her away from the war. I don't know why. Perhaps I'm scared to get too close to her. Maybe I think the full savage picture, the animal horror of it all, might shock her. Maybe I'm scared she'd think less of me. Maybe I don't want to get into it myself. So, instead, I tell her other stuff.

About my mother, dead when I was a kid. No memories there at all. Except our slum house in Bowden. No-hopersville. The smell of the SA gasworks close by. About my old man in his BSA and sidecar rushing off at all hours to fix up people's cars. He'd been quite proud of that job. It was the first regular one I can remember him having. Most of the time we were wandering about the countryside, Mum, me, and the Old Man, in a battered Morris ute, all our belongings piled up in the back. When we stopped it was in the Upper Murray for fruit picking or up in Queensland for cane cutting. We lived in these little shanties of corrugated iron the bosses had on their properties. They treated us like shit. They fired him from one place, Barmera, because he took time off to go in to the hospital to see Mum. That's where she died. I don't remember any of it. Anyhow he was proud of this regular job. Enjoyed it. On call all the time, off at any hour of the night. Kind of an unpredictable job for a restless bloke. And the weird people he encountered: The couple stuck together literally in the back seat of a Baby Austin, naked and embarrassed. They had to be carried out still locked together on one stretcher to the hospital. Yvonne doesn't think that's too funny. She doesn't like the way my old man went out, either, smashed between a broken-down Holden and a big Dodge truck up in the hills near Aldgate. Nor Croydon Primary School I went to, where the bastard chalkie caned you once on the hand for every spelling error in the weekly Friday tests. I used to rub horse liniment into my palms every Friday morning. I always got two or three wrong. She shakes her head at that brutality. Or Croydon Tech and the useless education I buggered off from at fourteen, fruit picking in the Murray with a bunch of no-hopers. Or the sheep stations, where I refused to go roo shooting one night and they put a dead doe in my bed while I slept and I had ringworm all over my body. That one nearly made her sick.

Or receiving the Birthday Bullet. The birthday draw for Vietnam, where they drew a number of dates from a barrel or something and if your birthday came up, you went. She can't understand why I went. But where the hell is there to run away to in Australia unless you can swim a thousand miles? And besides, at that stage, eighteen nearly nineteen, it looked like an adventure, and I'd bought all the male macho bullshit of the lean, tough, laconic bronzed Anzac since I was a kid. I know better now; that the Poms got us for two or three wars and the Yanks for a couple. We were a pushover.

She doesn't tell me much about her past. That's her business I reckon. She'll tell me one day. But she starts to pontificate about men and violence and I feel a real ripe anger building up, tell her I don't want to talk about it any more, but she's on about women and politics and the Crisis Centre and some battered woman with two black eyes and two kids and men and violence, and I have a flash of that village we came into where the mothers and kids were sprawled out and bloody, shot down in a heap for no good reason at all, by the VC or maybe us, who knows, and I get snarly and tell her she's full of shit, tell her to get out of my life, and she gets mad, and I spring out of bed, naked and shaking with anger at one A.M. and tell her to leave, to piss off, and she's cold and brittle and dresses and goes, and I walk the house all night, swigging rum and missing her so that the booze and lust double me up physically and I get drunk as a skunk and pass out. Why she goes on about the Crisis Centre I don't know. There's something about her she hasn't told me. But she rings the next morning as if nothing important has happened and I'm sorry and sick and down in my boots and she laughs and says it's okay, it's okay, and I wonder if I'll ever really be okay. I'm not used to being forgiven. I suppose that's love. I've been reading Shakespeare. It's one of the books Yvonne brought over for me. *Othello.* What I understand of it. Desdemona loved Othello because of his scars. Sounds like pity for an emotional cripple. I'm not sure. Is that what Yvonne thinks of me?

13

THE COCKATIEL STRUTS about the table pecking at images in the mirrored light of the varnished table. Unafraid, it patters close to where I sit, pencil in hand. It is a beautiful creature. The two black eyes, the light green crest that rises like a consciousness at interest, the slate grey feathers, laid like the petals of a flower so they merge into one another uniformly, the blush of pink/orange behind and below the eyes, the white-edged wings, the long spear of the tail, barred with yellow underneath, the hooked beak, the tongue round as a grub, the fine hooked claws. Where does all this come from? What evolutionary pattern marks the code with hollow wings and frail beauty designed for what? To do what? Whirr past our eyes in a fleeting glimpse of imagined form? Linked to what incredible chain of past events, to what miraculous consequences in what metaphysical or natural linking of desert, sun, seed, and distribution pattern.

The cockatiel starts. Flies up. Seconds later I hear the whomph, whomph of helicopter blades and into the bay flies a grey bird of another evolution, and below it, suspended in a net, a black cigar shape. I put the binoculars on it. Sure enough. A torpedo from the testing range out in Whiskey Gulf. They're getting ready for another war. Somewhere.

The cockatiel flies unassisted into its cage. I sit down and put this down for what it's worth. On paper.

14

I FIRST MET WACKER after his big bet had been neatly buggered up by a young cop in Ceduna.

I was nineteen. I'd been bagging wheat on a German's farm and bringing it twenty miles onto the siding just out of Ceduna in Thevenard. It was the last year before the bulk trucks took over; they were building the silos then. Wacker'd had his grader job out of Alice shut down when they put the new bitumen stretch of road in, and he was stacking wheat bags on the siding, getting good pay, but his heart wasn't in it. He missed the Red Centre. He'd grown up there and wanted to buy a cattle station somewhere north of Alice. We all had dreams.

Anyhow a couple of the older blokes lumping wheat bags on the siding were going on about Sid Harrison, how he'd thrown a wheat bag up on his shoulder, a year ago, run down to the Thevenard pub half a mile away, drunk a pint and got back to the gates of the siding in forty-two minutes without dropping it once. Wacker reckoned he could do that easy, so they got to bullshit and dare and he finally took the two blokes on for fifty bucks each that he could take two bags, one on each shoulder, drink a pint at the Thevenard and get back to the gates in half an hour. The word spread like top fire in mallee scrub. Everybody got in on the betting. The local SP bookie had Wacker at two to one, and I put ten bucks on him myself. Wacker was over six foot, but he looked thin, and he had a big long nose and red hair. He was all big bones and long muscles and tough as hell. I'd seen him plant his legs and throw a wheat bag up five feet, like it was a feather pillow.

We all came in to see the race on Saturday morning, even the German cockie bastard I was working for, though he was so tight he squeaked when he walked. He was so cheap he wouldn't have even bet on a sure thing like Phar Lap.

Right at noon, Wacker throws one bag up, gets the other put on his right shoulder, and he sort of crouches and runs out the gate and down the dirt road towards the Thevenard. Now a bag full of wheat is bloody heavy, dead weight you know, slippery, and hard to centre and keep stable. Two of them are more than double trouble because you can't lean in to keep the weight over your back and feet. But there's Wacker, both arms up around the wheat bags, half-crouching, but making good speed towards the Thevenard. And there's maybe a hundred or more people yelling and cheering on the sides of the road as he runs in that half-crouch, with the wheat bags bobbing about on his shoulders. Into the bar he goes. Marge, the barmaid, has his pint of Southwark all ready, and I race in to see. The clock reads 12:14. His time's tight. He winks, says, In your eye, and drains it. Marge starts yelling about paying, and Wacker stands a second, red faced with sweat pouring down his face. I nip in and pay the old tart.

Thanks, mate, he says, and he's off, pushing the pace a bit, knowing his time is thin as a razor's edge. The mob's following him now, all cheering and hollering and whoopeeing it until he gets ten yards from the gate, and there's this copper, young bloke just in from Adelaide, putting his hand up to stop Wacker. So he stops a second, panting away right in front of the copper.

That's Wheat Board property there, says the copper, tapping the bags.

She'll be right. I'm taking it back, says Wacker. C'mon I got a bet on this.

Sorry, says the copper. You better put them bags down, and come with me. Cries from the crowd. Piss off, copper. Let 'im finish it. Give 'im a go.

Wacker starts to move forward. The copper puts his hand on Wacker's chest. The copper's caught now. He can't let Wacker go through or he'll look piss weak. Everybody'll laugh at him. Stupid situation to get yourself into. Authority. All bullshit.

Fuck off, says Wacker. Seconds are ticking away.

Your name, says the copper, reaching into his breast pocket for a notebook.

Wacker's right fist flies suddenly forward, dongs the copper on his nose, sets him on his arse. Wacker gets his arm back just in time to save the right wheat bag from falling, steps over the fallen copper, and runs past the gates with twenty seconds to spare. The mob cheers, hats fly, the old-timers come forward to shake his hand. The woman from the *Ceduna Free Press* is taking a photo, the money's changing hands, it's a great day.

When up roars a cop car and four of the black-and-white bastards rush forward, grab Wacker, throw the cuffs on him, and try to push their way through the crowd. Now the mob's really pissed off; they're pushing and shoving the coppers, and two of the bastards pull out their billies and start flailing about; and then a few stones whizz by and the cops're lucky, the car is rocked and pummelled and six blokes lift the back up so the rear wheels just spin and rev, but finally it's like any time you try to buck the bosses, they can't hold it forever and Wacker's off to the clink.

I catch up with Wacker later that evening in the Thevenard. He's bruised and a bit bloodied from the thumping the cops have given him in the gaol. He's sipping his Southwark sideways with a puffed mouth.

What'd the beak give you? I ask, knowing that the judge just happened to be on circuit today. Probably why those brindle bastards of cops put on a show.

He gave me a choice, smiles Wacker through his busted up mouth, assault, resisting arrest, theft, and so on, about a year inside. Or Vietnam.

Buckley's eh? I offered.

Nah. Always did like travel, says Wacker, with this sardonic grin.

It was about six months later I got the Birthday Bullet myself. That was the gambling way the Australian government got its volunteers for Vietnam. A Birthday Clause. But I was glad to get away from that cheap German cockie.

He was pretty impressed. I wouldn't mind betting he had a swastika tattooed on his gotchees. Gave me a line about Queen and Country in his guttural spitting out of the English language, even pulled out a bottle of plonk, gave me a drink, and drove me in to the bus depot. Slipped me an extra five dollars. Shook my hand and drove off.

I looked over Ceduna as the bus pulled out. Corrugated iron, dusty roads, heat and dogshit. Who the hell'd ever miss a place like that? Vietnam? I didn't even know where it was.

15

IN ITS CAGE the cockatiel cackles as the snow flies outside the bay window. Like the soft shed breast feathers of a huge bird, the flakes settle a foot deep. Insanely, the cockatiel dances and twirls on the top perch as the thick feathers swirl; it finally hangs upside down and batters its wings wildly against the brass mesh. In their turn the tiny white breast feathers of the bird float softly about the room.

With its head under its grey wing, the cockatiel dreams of gliding in a flock over sunlit grass, wing feathers distended, the sun a white-hot ball overhead. The smell of water pulls the grey flock like a flecked shawl up and around the billabong, a circular glint of water in the red sandstone outcrop near Ayers Rock. A hundred or more birds, chattering and waddling up to the water, dipping their necks and raising them high to swallow. Parked half a mile away is the bird trapper's truck.

The rockets bang simultaneously, the net snakes high and wide and fast, so that few even get into the air and suddenly the flock of cockatiels are trapped, lie squirming like so many mice under the fine nylon mesh. Later they'll be flown over to the U.S. and sold. Half of them will die in the cages. It's like the black slaves from Africa.

Though I was young, the cockatiel observes from its cage, scratching one wattle pensively, I could perceive my family's flock as a notable society with simple and credible ends. The cockatiel works a sunflower seed back and across its beak so the shell drops empty to the bottom of the cage. Anarchism in its best form, confirms the cockatiel. No individual bothered another except for minor squabbles quickly resolved by height, weight, and strength. A brief skirmish and order was resumed. No continual conflict, or widespread violence whatsoever. No levelling by law or elevation by inheritance, no patronage, no sexism, no Machiavellian leers or lurks, no socialism. No bullshit democracy. Sadly, though, those fucking bird trappers had totally primitive capitalist perceptions.

16

HANGMAN, WACKER GROWLS AT ME from under hooded eyes. We lie naked in a boom-boom bar near the base. Hangman, he says, meaning hanging in to the last, one more beer too many as they say, creator of hangovers. The two Vietnamese girls giggle and begin counting the big freckles on Wacker's bare belly. Their little fingers twist the red hair sprouting like spinifex.

I feel sick in my body, in my mind. My head is spinning so that my eyes move independent of my will. I want to be elsewhere. Anywhere.

Hangman, snarls Wacker, look at the mess!

Outside a charred circle. Bits of uniform and webbing. I realize I am naked. I convinced Wacker last night that if we burned our uniforms, the gods would approve and set us free of the red mud and bamboo shit spikes. Jesus, we must have been blind pissed. At least the radio's still intact.

The smaller of the two girls comes over to me. Her breasts are no more than those of a fat boy's. I cannot remember her at all, though last night I had thrust with passion into her. It throws me.

You like suck? she says and bends over me. I feel like crying.

Hangman, says Wacker, standing up shakily, we have problems. His frame is bony, angular, hollow like a cow's rear end. Clothes, Hangman, think clothes. And think MPs and how the fuck we get back into camp. Think, Hangman, think.

I look about. There are only two dresses hanging on the

hooch's wall. They'll have to do. Oh no, Hangman, Wacker says sadly, following my gaze. Oh no.

But it is Sunday. We have to be back at camp.

So that's how we end up walking up to the camp sentry post at dusk, wearing dresses and broad straw hats. Great gangling bovine women with hairy legs, Wacker in black, me with a floral design on the dress, a radio hanging on my back. Harris is on duty. We are lucky. Known as a great trousers snake man, he looks about, beckons us on in, thinking to get a quick fuck before anybody notices. Harris is famous for his knothole philosophy. He reaches down to grope at what he thinks is a woman's groin and grabs instead a handful of Wacker's cock and balls. The recoil is instant. His lips turn up in horror. Want a quick one, sweetie? I call out in falsetto. Harris whirls about to look at me. What the hell are you two doing in that get-up? he cries. Finally come out of the closet, eh. Well bugger me. You had me fooled. But, Jesus, you're so ugly, he laughs. You'd have to pay me!

Wacker snarls and grabs his throat.

You stupid bastard, Harris, you'd let some Vietnamese pussy in here and get us all killed!

Easy Wacker, I cry. Take it easy.

Of course, up turns Double Barrel, just at that precise moment, Lieutenant Smith-Creighton RAR, wondering what the noise is. His voice chokes, and his Adam's apple has a bobbing fit when he sees us in dresses, with Wacker's hand around Harris's throat. There's a bit of a silence. How do we explain this one?

It's like the time I was up at Woodside with a sheep-brained sergeant training us on some old Bofors gun, running us ragged to get us to set up and fire the old bucket of nuts and bolts in twelve seconds. And the silence when one of the new recruits pointed out the Bofors was obsolete in 1947 and that the Viet Cong didn't have jet fighters anyway. It was that kind of silence when they're gathering the shit in truck loads on high just waiting for the exact moment to let it all tip down on you.

Double Barrel, not knowing what to do, or say for that matter, gargles out something like, What's going on here?

Suddenly inspired I yell out something like, Counterinsurgency, sir. In disguise, sir.

Oh, says Double Barrel, very well. Carry on. And in obvious mental disarray, he turns and stalks off. Officer behaviour you know, not like the sergeant in charge of the Bofors, who had every last mother's son of us, after the new recruit's comments, run many laps in full gear, had us make out loud the noises of imagined Viet Cong fighter jets attacking and the noises of our Bofors gun shooting down every last one of them, and the explosions when they hit the ground, in chorus, and a rousing cheer for every one of our successful twelve-second shots. Now, that's the real army way. Drama. Imagination.

Anyhow, Wacker lets go of Harris's throat and Harris whips off to get us some army gear and we return to normal soldiering. Except that Double Barrel has that strange look in his eye the next morning when he sees us, as if there's some weird sexual perversity abroad he doesn't want to know about. Maybe it's a St. Peter's College special, dressing like girls, and he's scared we've found out.

17

THE COCKATIEL FLUTTERS OVER, reads what I've just written and shakes its wattles.

I don't believe that, the bird announces.

That's what happened, I say, shrugging my shoulders. I feel like slowly strangling the feathered freak. But there's no point in letting him get to me. I know what happened. I was there. That's what matters. Not what the cockatiel or anybody says.

Factuality is irrelevant, you poltroon, states the cockatiel flatly. Clearly this is not fiction but anecdote. No one would be willing to suspend disbelief for a second.

The bird flies off.

Well, that throws me. I'll have to ask Yvonne about that one. What's the difference? How can you know?

Damn it, I'm bloody sick of living with an instant ever-ready critic like the cockatiel. I wonder if other writers have the same problem. Of course not. The cockatiel is a unique monster.

Worse than that, the damn bird is growing so psychologically huge, this cabin isn't big enough for the two of us. I liked it better when it just sat and hopped about its cage and was silent. Now it's almost out of control. Its presence pushes me into a corner. I'm constantly defending myself. Or I'm at its constant beck and call.

The cockatiel demands now more than seed. Apricots, almonds, french toast, bananas, cashews. Caviar, it whispered at my ear last night, and Russian grey not the cheap Canadian substitute, and a sip, if you please, of Dom Perignon.

Who is this cockatiel? What lurks in its light and hollow bones, its moulded grey pinions? The yellow patch and red circle below its black eyes, its passionate small heart, its greedy beak and grasping claws. It could be human. It's no drongo. Probably the bastard's smarter than me. But it's a real pain to live with. Maybe his comments make more sense than I like to admit. Examine your true feelings, Yvonne always says, below what you think you should feel. It's hard to do, but I try. Do I really hate this bird? Some of the time. Do I like it? No. Not really. Would I miss it if it flew away? Yes. I look at it again. It cocks its head high as if in some exquisite intellectual anguish. It could be human.

18

I THINK IT WAS just after the tiger incident that Wacker started to lose it. You could accept a lot of chaos, a lot of carnage, blood and dead bodies, but it was the sheer raving madness of what they made us do that finally started to pop inside you. Great periods of boring stupid slogging over and over the same terrain, endless hours of rice paddies, high grass, jungle, marsh, dykes, and then a few seconds or a minute of shooting and explosions and screams and terror and then back to the slogging away. Or a sniper, wham, or a booby trap, and someone near you falls with half a leg, half a face, half an arm blown into bits. Or the troop carrier we came upon, split right in halves by a road mine, torn steel still smoking, and inside, two Aussies, blown apart, legs and arms separate and gory, and one bloke, the driver I reckon, without a scratch, with his headphones still on, staggering about aimlessly, muttering, Fucking hell, oh fucking hell. But it was going out on patrol with the Yanks we hated most.

They'd be on patrol, yakking and clanking and smoking—anybody'd pick up that tobacco smoke a quarter of a mile away. And the shouting and the bickering. Anyhow, we went out one afternoon to set up a big block or ambush on a trail in some light jungle and grass two miles out. Supposed to be a big batch of NVA and supplies coming through at night. Take back the night. I remember reading that some women were protesting with that written on placards. We could've used those signs. The night belonged to the Viet Cong. All of them. Working in the fields, women and kids too. Jekyll and Hyde. The kid you tossed a

Wrigley's spearmint gum to in a village could be the same kid who tossed a grenade at you that night. The little girl selling stolen Coke cans could watch you walk right onto a land mine. It was sick.

So there we are waiting for the Yanks to turn up at our jump-off point and we hear this booming noise. We scatter. Then down the track come about a hundred Yanks, yakking, smoking, drinking Coke, and damn it, there are two tanks, grinding away, diesels roaring. Peace signs and graffiti on the tanks. The Yanks are wearing all sorts of weird gear: red bandanas, peace badges, headbands, long hair, beads. A lot of them are blacks, a lot of backslapping, grinning, handslapping, jumping about.

What the fuck? says Wacker, standing up.

Element of surprise? I offer with irony.

Christ, they'll hear us miles away, Wacker says, I don't like it.

He's not good on irony. He walks towards the Yanks.

Lieutenant Double Barrel is already there chatting away. Wacker comes back. Don't ask, he says. We move out. Wacker keeps us well to the rear. It's hot. It rains. We sweat.

Stupid bastards, he tells me finally. Their lieutenant tells Double Barrel that if the tanks travel in low gear no one'll hear them. It's a travelling bloody circus. Even Double Barrel works that one out and finally comes back to the rear with us. Maybe he is learning.

We set up, dig in as far away from the tanks as we can. Sitting ducks. They're covered with foliage but I can still smell the diesel and their food. And the Yanks cooking and squabbling like kids as the sun sets. Finally it all quietens down. Like most of the time, nothing much happens. We get our Nog line out, cans on fishing line, Claymores. I sleep. Get woken at two A.M. and look out. Rain. Clearing. Jungle. Clearing. You have to be careful or your eyes make shapes, then make the shapes move.

All of a sudden there's this scream from the Yanks. Tiger. Tiger. They're all up and running for the tanks. Clong. Whang. Clang. The tank turrets are swung open. A flare goes off and there's twenty of them running for the safety of the tanks, fighting to get in. Brrp. The tank's diesels start up. Their officer's yelling at them.

We're all awake and tense. A great dark barred beast comes flying from one side. Christ—a tiger. I turn to shoot, but up it leaps, scared shitless at the noise no doubt, and in two bounds it's gone. The Yanks scurry about. A bunch of them slowly climb out of the tanks again. The tanks' engines are turned off.

Wacker is livid. I can hear his jaws grinding in the dark. Double Barrel starts to crawl off to see the Yank officer, but he's getting smarter and thinks better of it. Good chance they'd shoot him right now.

There's noise and intermittent bickering all night. When we pull out in the morning we run into a whole bunch of tracks two hundred yards behind us. That's what the NVA'd done. A simple detour around a bunch of noise. We hadn't heard a thing. And all because some Yanks got freaked by a tiger. As if the bloody tiger'd do anything like the harm VC could. The bloody animal was probably shit scared that it had run into us, anyhow.

Wacker is very pissed off. There's all these men and supplies we might've got last night. But it's not just that. It's his pride. And it's even worse when Double Barrel, the pride of St. Peter's, volunteers us to follow the tracks for a bit, while the Yanks wend their noisy chaotic way safely back to their base. I don't want to follow any tracks, anywhere. Wacker doesn't. Harris and the rest also think it's insane. It's exactly what the Nogs'd expect. They'd have to have an ambush set up, expecting the Yanks'd follow their tracks.

Double Barrel's going on about duty. We turn our backs on him. Wacker takes Double Barrel away from us a little way. They argue. We all get this seething, angry feeling. A killing mood. I reckon I'll see a repeat of Thevenard and the cop with Wacker. But we don't. They come back. We slog. But not on the path. We move in two lines, a hundred yards on either side of the trail they've left. Double Barrel, though, walks down the track. A reluctant Harris follows him twenty yards behind carrying the radio.

We slog through grass, through this light jungle. It rains. We get wet. The sun pushes through. We steam. Up to the little ridge. Double Barrel's ahead. We see him stop. He turns to wave Harris up. Dukduk, dukduk. Half of Double Barrel's face flies away in blood. Harris spins and falls. I feel the bile rising to my throat. Swallow it. Two down. No more fire. We edge up to the ridge. Half a mile off in a little valley stand a dozen thatched huts in four or five acres of rice paddy. Wacker crouches, runs to the bodies, falls flat. They're both dead. Wacker, dragging the radio, comes back. His face is white and splotched with anger. He's gone over the edge.

Wack, I say, let's back off. Let the Yanks have this one. It's their zone.

Fuck it, he spits, we go in.

We come into the village in a fan. Run and fall. Run and fall. It's stupid, I keep hearing myself say. They're going to open up any minute. Stupid. But there's no movement at all from the huts. They've seen us. They're all inside hiding. Off to my right, Wacker's fire zone, a figure in black runs for the jungle at the edge of the rice paddy. Wacker drops it in two shots. Flop. Shudder of black. An AK opens up from near one of the huts. Little Sam yells, I'm hit, Christ I'm hit. We blast the hut. Stillness again.

We leapfrog into the village, pull all the chattering, crying Vietnamese out of their huts into a kneeling mob. How many times have I done this, seen it done. Poke and prod. Fearful grins. Rotten teeth. Smell of fish and shit. We search the huts. Nothing. But in the rafters, Anderson finds half a dozen AK47s hidden in the thatch of one hut. Clever, layered in. Wacker takes the two men from the hut with the AKs out by a rickety pig stall. They're wearing singlets and black shorts. So skinny they look like kids. He beats them down flat onto the ground with two vicious swings of his rifle butt. They lie squirming. One bleeds.

Hey, Wacker, I yell running up to him, hang on.

He turns a face to me I've never seen before. A vicious mask. White and red. I know he'll shoot me. I stop.

He yells at them. VC! VC! They shake grinning faces at him. He fires a shot between them into the ground. They writhe in terror. The pigs squeal and dash about.

VC! Wacker yells, VC! More shakes of their heads.

Fucking bastards! Wacker screams. He fires again and the backs of the heads of two Vietnamese fly apart like dropped watermelon. I'm shit scared. Wacker calms down.

We call in. The Yank choppers fly in. They find a tunnel entrance. Probably dozens of Nogs down there. They look around for someone to go down and winkle them out, like a ferret going after rabbits, holding a .45 and a torch. I tried it once and freaked out. The whole country is probably honeycombed with tunnels. The Nogs just pop up like rabbits, take a quick shot and disappear. They've got whole cities we can't find burrowed underneath us. It's a hopeless fucking war. The Yank captain calls in a special team. They blow acetylene gas down the tunnel into the warren and explode it. No one knows if it works.

The dust-off chopper comes in. We carry Little Sam—bloody chest, white eyes—to a chopper. Slapping, pushing and shoving, the South Vietnamese Rangers take the villagers away. We squat and watch. It's like a TV show you've seen too many times, except there's no switch to turn it off. The choppers coming and going, the screams and squeals and shouts as the villagers are shoved into the helicopters, their thatched huts burning now, explosive charges booming in their rice caches. It's like the Nazi movies. Kids crying. Mothers screaming. They all just disappear. The two Vietnamese are left where they died. No questions. No one gives a fuck. Back home, they gave us lectures on the difference between normal combat casualties and murder. What a bunch of officer bullshit. There's no difference here.

Another Yank chopper picks up Double Barrel and Harris from the ridge where they lie in congealed blood.

We walk out up the ridge. It's just after noon. Wacker takes us down the trail. We're all sick in the guts of this chaos. Fuck the war. I see Double Barrel's head fly into pieces again and again, Harris pirouetting as his knees buckle. The two villagers' heads bust apart.

I catch up to Wacker.

Byzantine, he's muttering, striding out fast. Over and over again he mutters, Byzantine.

19

THE IMMELMANN TURN, intones the cockatiel from the mantelpiece, was designed to outfox the classic nose-to-tail form of air combat in 1916. If, for example, I am a Sopwith Camel diving and rolling to get away from you on my tail in your Fokker triplane, I'm in big trouble, because your three-winged plane has greater lift and mobility. So I pull the Immelmann and I'm tat-tat-tat, tat-tat-tat, firing short bursts at deflective angles not where you are but where you'll be in that split second that the tracer arrives. This, of course, was Buzz Buerling's great ability in Malta.

C'mon, I say.

Similarly, the cockatiel continues, ignoring me, the three gladiators on Malta—Hope, Faith, and Charity—survived in World War II because of their greater mobility in the air though they were 250 miles per hour slower than the Macchis or Messerschmitts they came up against. Or shall I discuss the Harriers in the Falklands War?

You're full of it, I say.

Ignoramus, snarls the cockatiel leaning forward, its beak snapping. You couldn't hit a barn door!

Want to bet? I ask, holding up a nerf ball.

I can outfly anything in the air, cries the bird, launching into flight, zooming across the living room, darting, hovering, dropping, wings closed to the floor, zigzagging in bursts of wings, flaps, and deceptive twists until it comes to my face, hovers. Try it, Richthofen, just try it, the bird hisses and is off again about the room.

My first two throws miss by at least a foot. The bird cackles and bursts about the room. I hold onto the third throw with the nerf ball until the bird is close to the window . . . left turn I guess, and heave the soft sponge. Now, the ball would have missed the bird except for a spectacular flick and loop the cockatiel pulls and poof, runs right into the ball and falls fluttering to the carpet. I feel sick. The bird's so frail. The flesh is so frail. A bullet tears it to shreds. And there's the bird lying crumpled on the living room floor.

Lucky shot, you shit, curses the cockatiel as I rush to pick it up. Christ, my neck feels like it's broken.

20

MAZE. AMAZE. Miss Maze 1970. That's what Wacker's ribbed sole looks like. Does the soul also have these curved cleats, these treads for traction in desperate straits? The grass waves above us, ignores us, our questions. Or is sin like the knobs on the liver, the black nicotine spots on the lungs; is it sin that sears and scours the original smooth seventeenth-century surface of the soul, weaving such rivers and chasms and gullies that the earth is subject to in its decay? That we wander in this entropy looking for the way out.

He doesn't move a muscle. The boot splays out in the grass, the tops of which sway and bend in the varying breeze. The handle, black bound leather, of his illegal throat knife in its sheath within the boot, looks small and fragile. We wait for some chattering or maybe silent small men with rifles like ours to stumble into our trap. We are a living maze for their death. They will lose their breath in our cunning, in our amaze of death.

The maze of the sole in his boot. Its shapes. The outer circle of treads like edges of pie leading to the multifoliate rose within. A star. A cross of many colours. Follow these tracks men. He must be the ringleader. Six multifoliate inner treads. I will consider these part of a web we spin, are spun into. My body is numb. We could be here forever. Waiting. We could sink into the earth, grass up our arses. Months later, they died of inaction, grass grew into them, through their sphincters, bones, eyes. They forgot how to stand. They forgot how to move. They became one with the shit and the heat and the rice paddies. They forgot how to get the hell out of here. How to live.

Behind us, in a little stand of rubber trees, the five Vietnamese we caught sleeping, eating, shitting in their bunker, have been extended the horrible mercy of our Vietnamese ranger advisor. He has an exquisite and refined sense of cruelty. I tried to stop him, but Wacker put his arm out, grabbed my shirt front, pushed me away.

They are wired up. Thin wire. In a circle. The wire thrust through one's joined hands, cheeks, tongue then through the tiny penis and up to the next one's hands, cheeks, tongue, and cock. They bow in a crouch head down, as if they are praying, absolutely still. Any movement by any one of them rips the soft flesh. Little drops of blood form at their feet in a circle. The ranger pulls out a grenade, makes as if to leave it at their feet. They cry out, but cannot move. Frozen in pain and fear. The ranger laughs. It makes me sick. I want to shoot the sad fucker. I'm shocked but fascinated. The symmetry of horror. This shape is another nationality type. Wacker comes up with them. A bore of Poms. A yawn of Canadians. A brash of Americans. An outrage of Australians. What will this be? Wacker'll come up with it. Something like a cockwire of Cong. We're all transfixed by it. We all watch this pain.

Byzantine, I hear myself muttering.

Let's go. Wacker moves among us, patting and tapping shoulders and arms.

We move out. To be frozen ourselves shortly, in the high grass, in ambush, tied one to each other in the thin thrill of fear and anticipation. We wait.

My mind has been wandering. I glance at my watch: 2:30. My mouth is dry; my hands and face sweat. I dare not reach for my canteen. Before the ranger wired them up they said the VC'd be here by early morning. Probably lying. But they have to come back this way. Have to link up with this base camp. I'm half-asleep.

The first mortar hits behind us, fifty yards. Pomph. I hear the second coming. And the third. How the hell have they got us tagged? More likely it's friendly fire. Some dumb Yank thinks we're VC.

Back out. Sideways, yells Wacker, galvanized now. Keep low.

My guts are a knot. My sphincter opens. How did they know? Fuck it. Out. Get out. Out of here.

I scrabble and crawl as fast as I can. The air seems alive with moaning, whirring insects. We are four rats side by side, scurrying for our holes.

I am lifted, soul, body, mind, high in a crush of air.

I glide into growing darkness.

21

FREEDOM! OUT THERE? In that frozen waste? With those savages? Is that what you offer? The cockatiel refers here to the crows that daily fly past the bay window, to his unintelligible curses and insults. They're just out of the trees! Do you think I want that illusion! The slings and arrows of outrageous fortune? Not to mention kids with pellet guns, lickspittle cannibal cats, dogs of low IQ, and marauding hawks and eagles. Freedom? Forget about Blake and his silly bird in a cage sets heaven in a rage. Or is it Rousseau, you deluded fool? Noble Nature? Noble Savages? Wordsworth? Rejuvenation? Mummy Nature? Bambi? Hell no. It's dog eat dog out there and no place for a bird. Think you'd satisfy some romantic guilt by getting me off your hands? Forget it! Why did Lucky stick with Pozzo? Friday with the Man? The slave is father of the masters. Oh give me a role with no romantics so droll.

The bird rocks on its perch to that tune, and for ending raises its tail for the now familiar salute.

22

BUT WHAT are you going to do with your life? Yvonne's question hangs in the air. She adds a nervous crazy laugh to it. An unsettling giggle that throws me. I hate the thought of answering, the idea of a plan, a chart. Objectives, weekly, monthly. It's what she always does to me. Points the finger. More like points the bone. It's what I love in her. It's also what I hate, can hardly stand, this probing, as if she wants to get inside. Sometimes I feel like one of those oysters the crows pick up on the beach here. They fly high and drop them, pick them up and drop them on the rocks till they crack and the soft insides ooze out. I can't drop my shell. But that's not being fair. I couldn't live without Yvonne. Now. Yes, I could survive, but that's not living. I'm more alive than I ever was. She's got me reading everything. Thinking. Discussing things. Before Yvonne, I was a savage. That's what Conrad said, before the Congo I was a savage. A weird comparison I know, Yvonne and the Congo, but I reckon he meant he didn't look at himself, get a bit of a glimmer at what made him tick. That's what Yvonne has done, despite the cockatiel and its bullshit intellectualism. She's the one who's brought the books, made me think and read and reflect. Made me grow.

She is full, round, and sweet. Appley, you might say, as in apples, her apple breath, her sweet gloss and sweeter inside. Ah, the temptation. Her excellent sweet and apple, or her breath sweeter than apple cider, inside her, I become a fly in the cider of her thighs.

She sits there now, white blouse, long dark skirt, barefoot, leaning back in her chair. Talk to me, O'Donnell, she says. She expects an answer. There isn't one. She makes me feel cynical. I know she's naive. She couldn't conceive the mindless mess of bodies burst open, blown apart and the endless blood. Is this what Conrad's talking about too? Keep it from the women at all cost? Tell her lies to save her from the blood and guts of Vietnam? She was frightened too, the first night we were in bed. After the dream came I woke up thrashing about on the floor, looking for my rifle. Same old situation. You'd think after all this time I'd be able to laugh it off. But I can't. The same vague spinning threat suddenly falling, whistling out of the sky, a grenade, a mortar, I don't know except that it has the round bronze flash and sharp edges of a huge penny, like a scythe reaping all before it. I roll and twist and scuttle away but it follows, curving, turning, its edges sharp and ominous until I wake up.

She was scared that first night, cried a bit herself. Jumped out of bed as if I was going to hit her, but she held me and I slept after that. But the dream still bounces back, as if to say, Hey, remember me, mate? Yvonne tells me she has dreams a bit like that, too.

And the other dream. The black Mercedes pulls up and five young men with faces like Wacker's and mine are pulled out, forced to kneel and then shot. The bullet comes out twisting very slowly from the barrel and I begin to scream as it enters my head and explodes ever so slowly, ever so dramatically.

It's in bed that we get along best. She is chubby and bouncy and breathless making love. We do not fuck, she says, we make love, there is a big difference. I'm not yet convinced, but I keep my mouth shut about that, though she is a loud and lusty wench, given to cries and crudities, even throaty screams, so that I stopped once, thinking I was hurting her, and she gasped and laughed, No, no I'm fine, and got me going straight away with magnificent shimmying thrusts of her hips. Once, as I explored the cider inside her thighs she was so wound up and thrashing she broke wind, and cried and laughed. She flushed red with embarrassment and had an orgasm all at the same bewildering emotional instant. She was wiped out after that. But not enough to stop asking questions. Probing. Interested. She can't believe my life. The hard work picking, farming, driving; the money I blew gambling, on horses, two-up games, casinos, poker. It's a foreign, bizarre way to live for her. I suggest that her existence on grants year after year is no different, but she shakes her head and smiles. She doesn't smile when we talk about previous lovers. She's had four. That includes one black bloke from Jamaica she fucked for a while but never loved, she says. Ah, there's the distinction. I didn't know, couldn't recall how many, who, names, places. She seemed upset when I couldn't remember my first full sexual experience. Damned if I can even remember it now. All that seems to fade into anonymous faces, unknown flesh. She remembers vividly, asks me if I'm jealous, and I am a bit, a lot about the first bastard, some twenty-year-old university law student in Toronto she got started with, all blond, a track star and A student. Like Double Barrel. I probably would have, I know I would have, hated the bastard, even without ever meeting him. She has some strange thing about that guy. I sense it. Perhaps he's still on her mind. Though I'm very cool and wise and detached when she mentions him. But show 'em how you feel and they've got you. So I pretend disinterest.

I don't think I'll like her family if I ever meet them, though there's fat chance of that. Her father in the photo, almost a caricature, grey hair and moustache, wearing a double-breasted suit, an art investor for Christ's sake, makes a bundle out of buying and selling paintings, antique clocks, and sculpture in Toronto, though he's retired and only dabbles in it a bit now, plays golf, has a five handicap, lives with her mother, a tall, grey-haired, round-faced woman with long, hippy hair, a gardener, you guessed it, organic, alternative, writes books and articles on health. Jesus, the talent in this mob. Shows in the big white two-storey house in Simcoe, Ontario, near the lake, with wrought iron gates. How the hell would I fit in there? The boy from the bush. And her brother, David, not Dave, five years older, is a bloody lawyer in some big firm in Toronto, athletic prick, tennis, racquetball, sailing, rich as shit, I gather, hobnobs with MPs and other right-wing assholes and argues tirelessly with his lefty sister. Though he sends her money and bought the bloody van she drives, cheap prick. I wonder what he'll think of the dink from Down Under, lowest on the social list, gambling nut, whose only skill is his hands and no great achievement there either, a bit of farming, a bit of bricking, a bit of flying chips and largely stuff all, except for the skill, courtesy of Her Majesty's

Australian Armed Forces and various purple-veined sergeants, courtesy of hands-on courses in the muggy climates of South East Asia, yes, the skill to kill.

Yvonne has no idea about Vietnam. I now don't want to push it, either. Though occasionally, her tales from the Crisis Centre, of brutality, of the frustrated males, jobless, lost egos swimming in beer parlour urinals, coming home to see the very image of their inadequacy, lashing out in dumb animal self-hate, seem sad, not violent. She has learned very quickly not to offload too much of that on me. I react badly, mindlessly. I cannot accept the relevance. All I see is the abattoirs, the mashed flesh and bone, the innocent bodies blown apart as if that, too, is daily bread.

It's the same with her tai chi. She dances it smoothly, powerfully. She talks a lot about the centre. Centre of energy. Centre of self. The power involved. It's a bit thick. She tells me about the bowl at the bottom of her belly, how she can concentrate and fill it, by breathing it in and down. And the delicate ball of balance she holds in imagined suspense in the triangular forces of her arms and legs. I have to work hard not to laugh. It's funny how you take bullshit from someone you like, how you just accept parts of the weird elements so you can have the whole person. I'm sure that's what she's doing with me. That's what I try to do with her. Live with the dumb bits, but it's not easy. There's something a bit weird about her. A kind of craziness she hides. Last night she comes up to me, teasing, dares me to attack, keeps pushing, gently, but insistently, her hands crossed, her body in a tai chi crouch. I ignore her until she slaps me twice, three times. Kidding, sneering, at the big male. Cut it out, Yvonne, I cry. I'm getting scared. She's acting crazy. I don't know why. Is she mad at me? What's going on? Is she testing me? I tell her to lay off. But she comes in again, faster, her arms whirling, yells, O'Donnell, you male bastard, and suddenly I lose it, go red alert for a second or two, have her down hard on the carpet, her hands locked, her head back, and then I catch myself, cursing, sit back and put my head on my knees, feeling ashamed and disgusted at what I know I can do, would do to anyone, that horror bred in Vietnam, to survive, survive, and fuck the rest.

And she crawling over me crying and neither of us understanding what happened even then, and both of us hugging each other and rocking like a pair of babies on the damn carpet. And I ask her, Why? Why did you do that? You knew what'd happen. Why did you do that? But she's totally silent. She won't say a damn thing. I think about dragging it out of her, but shit, I don't really care.

I just want to be left alone.

Do I love her? I don't know what love is. I've had it with all those words, love, honour, duty. It's like Hemingway's character says, all those abstractions are masks for slaughter. She thinks I'm afraid of love. She's probably right. It's hard to think someone like her, educated, middle class, well dressed, intelligent, beautiful, could get hooked up with a scary freak like myself, living on the edge. She says it's because I'm transparent, totally real. I don't understand it. Or her occasional craziness. But I don't show it. Or maybe it's because I don't want to lose someone again, keep up the guard in case the kiss-off comes, the See ya, Yeah, it's been a slice. Maybe I'm a battered male, all emotional scars, like she says, like one of these hockey players, crisscrossed with tiny white puck marks. Maybe she's my crisis centre. Maybe she needs me. I don't know. I'm not sure I care.

23

GZOWSKI SAYS ON CBC they've banned a book in Chilliwack. Must be a hell of a place, cries the cockatiel dancing on its perch as I enter from my morning walk. Get it! I must read it! Ah. Damn the black hoods of the Inquisition. My soul is my own, Ah to risk damnation. To know! To know! Ah sweet Helen. The cockatiel trails off into closed-eye bliss, dry kissing sounds emerging from its cracked beak. The transistor hangs with its earpiece jammed between the bars of the cage.

I turn on the radio in the kitchen. It's *Hustler* magazine, pulled off the shelves of drugstores in decent downtown Chilliwack, B.C.

I try to explain to the cockatiel that it's not important, but it rages and rants in its cage and demands, demands in shrieks and tirades against my shallow brain, ancestry, pitiful upbringing and so on, until it lapses into puffed and furious silence, its head stuffed determinedly under its wing.

I drive to the local 7-Eleven store. As I suspect, no one has heard anything there and *Hustler* stands in the top row of magazines. Of course it's still like buying condoms at sixteen from a chemist shop. The woman at the checkout turns the magazine around so the girl on the cover, naked, except for a huge lollipop strategically placed, is facing her. I'm embarrassed. The checkout woman says $3.95. I think I hear a tone of disapproval.

At home, the cockatiel flies to his reading perch and turns the glossy pages with trembling claws. The bird's transfixed by the centrefold, mesmerized, mumbling, as its head turns rhythmically side to side for a closer, deeper look.

Yes, the bird says, they're moving away from the full-figured Renaissance nude. Very interesting artistically, of course.

You lying bastard, I laugh, you're just a rotten pervert.

I assure you, intones the bird, that I read magazines like this mainly for the high-quality fiction found in them.

Pull the other leg, I chortle, it plays "Waltzing Matilda."

I grab the magazine. There are some photos of half-robed Asian women apparently tied up with rope, artfully exposing little bits of flesh. You can see the ropes aren't real; the women are acting. So who's having who on? The women? The male readers? Who's pretending what? Who's paid for what? It's one of these sex and money and power conundrums. It's pretty stupid stuff; only play violence. I've seen a lot worse than that in real, bloody, living colours. And no one gave a damn.

24

I PULL MY FINGERS DOWN from the top of the cage just in time as the guard rakes the FN rifle butt along the bamboo and giggles. I call him Elmer Fudd. We play a game. I am a circle of pain. I try to ease the forced fetal position by pulling up on the top of the cage. He tries to catch and break my fingers. Ironically, it is my rifle he uses. The heat dances like a red and black fish in my eyes.

They bring Wacker back from what they call an interview. Only this time he is hobbling horribly, falls, and is dragged to his feet, which are bloodied and swollen immensely. The pain is marked in the grin on his face, in the angular joints of his lips, as he staggers to the row of bamboo cages. We have all been bonsaied, like trees, made to crouch like animals, bow, become small, insignificant, subject to the power of our small captors, who now wear parts of our uniforms, carry our weapons, and stride tall about us. We have nothing to tell them, but it does not matter. Once a day in broken English they interview us up at the "office," focussing on one part of our bodies at a time. The questions are irrelevant. So are the answers. We know no generals, have no insight into plans or master strategies. We are tiny pairs of hands and arms in a surrealistic movie. Today they have mashed Wacker's feet. My turn will be next. The next cage. The next pair of feet. They are ready. It is methodical, unimaginative, effective.

They take greater delight in punishing Wacker. He is too tall for the tiny bamboo cage and is now jammed with blows and rifle butts down into a crouch where all the knobs of his backbone and neck bulge white with the strain. He cannot move. Giggling, they bang the cage top up and down, and the bamboo bars smash into his unprotected back until it is finally secured.

Fudd slips the bamboo bar across Wacker's cage, rattles the rifle butt across my cage, nearly gets my left hand, and walks down the row of cages looking for amusement. Later he will lean against a tree and light a cigarette. The safety's off, whispers Wacker. The blood drips slowly down from his immobile nose, plop, two, three, four plops. The safety's off. Fudd's rifle. My rifle. What it means is a quick grab at the trigger as Fudd is raking at my hands—and then what? The barrel pointing at his head. Blows it off. Misses? Too much luck involved. We mess it up. He shoots us. I'm not game enough to try it. Fear is so real. I prefer to dream. Movies. *Casablanca* . . . But out of the corner of my eye I see Wacker twisting his arm to get his left hand up. His back bulges against the bamboo bars. The pain is impossible. But there it is. A huge, bloodied left hand up at the top bars, the middle finger waving indecently. I see the freckles and the hair golden in the light.

When I grab the stock, he whispers, get the trigger. Fudd has seen it, the impertinent outrageous finger. He lets out a stream of abuse and runs back down the row of cages. I see the rifle raised to crush the hand, once, it grazes, twice, and Wacker grabs the stock, pulls, and slowly, immeasurably slowly, here life is slow motion, a replay on TV. As detached as Fudd. And the rifle tugs down, slowly down, and I reach, no, stab at the trigger with my right, once, twice, slowly hit the trigger guard, and suddenly Bang, Bang, one shot misses, the other takes Fudd's shoulder off, a strange, disproportionate event; the hole glows in the light. He falls, screaming, and amazingly we move the rifle between us, sideways, into the cage, across, and Wacker holds the muzzle up against the locking bar. I pull the trigger. Blast. And Wacker bursts up out of his cage—rises like a wondrous avenging angel, the light behind him religious, incandescent—pulling the rifle up by the barrel. Hops on bloodied feet along the row, smashing the lock bars, and one by one we jack-in-a-box up, bloody faced, Charlie Chaplin men in this movie, unsteadily out of the primeval crouch. Like we're all suddenly popped up out of the womb.

Run, he screams, run. He turns and fires at the four guards

running down from the office towards us. Two give that funny, flop-armed fall into the earth. Two others dive sideways into cover. Behind us, the rest of the prisoners scurry, crawl, limp, and run into the jungle.

C'mon! I grab Wacker's arm. He does not move. We are behind a tree. Wacker tears off his lucky penny. Shoves it in my hand.

No, I say.

Grenades! Wacker whispers. I scuttle to Fudd's body. He looks silly and adolescent in death. I strip the grenades. Wacker points left and right of the path. I cannot trust my arm overhead. I toss them underarm, right, left, and fling myself to the ground. Something flies up with the explosion and dust to the right. An arm? A branch?

C'mon! Urgently, I grab Wacker. He points to the extra clips around Fudd's waist. I get them. Wacker turns to me. Blood has dried in weird markings on his face, under his eyes, in the lines about his mouth. It's like war paint.

I got no feet to walk with, he grins savagely. You go.

I look again at his feet. Swollen like white bloody balloons, baroque, like a Disney cartoon.

I'll carry you, I cry, I can't leave you here.

Fuck that, spits Wacker, reaching for another clip.

I grab his arm, duck my head and shoulder under his chest, try to get him in the fireman's grip. I'm panicking. I want to get the Christ out of here. They'll shoot us for sure, this time. But my strength has gone, and we both crumple to the ground. Wacker lurches to his knees. I see the black hole of the rifle barrel six inches from my eyes. It's like a snake, wavering ever so slightly. I'm petrified.

Fuck off, he says, quietly, evenly, deliberately. I know he's going to shoot me if I don't. One great kerplash between the eyes. He's gone nuts. The grin on his bloody face is horrible. He's on a trip somewhere in his mind, some place I can't go.

Di di ma, Wacker spits. Fuck off!

I stand up, take two steps backward. The rifle barrel follows me.

I'll come back for you, I say.

You bet, he says.

I bloody will, I say.

I'll be here, he grins again. A bloody faced mask. Turns his attention back to where the guards disappeared. A burst of fire smacks in the thick foliage overhead.

I splash through the stream at our backs and into the jungle on the other side.

I run.

25

I AM NOT SURE what to do about Yvonne. It is always the same situation. I have to write down what happened. She just wants to talk. The two are mutually exclusive. To write requires that you take people and events at your own need, irregularly, inconstantly. It is selfish, self-seeking, unrelenting. To love means the hands. The words. Dishes. Potato peelings. Vacuuming. The detritus of daily feeding and washing, constantly, emotionally the getting down and grunging out the daily domestic details in the harness of love.

What would stop you from writing? Yvonne asks in that aggressive tone, searching my face for denial, acceptance, rejection, the signals of love.

O'Donnell, she says flatly, you're a selfish shit.

I just can't, I say, with anybody in the house. It just doesn't work. It's not the truth. I'm just wary of her, of getting too close in case I get hurt.

Oh! She expels her breath in a gesture of anger, disgust, disbelief and turns away from me. She has that curly dark red dust hair—an oval Botticelli face. Who wouldn't love her? She has stickers on her van for every cause. Cripples, MS, seals, peace, whales, education, Natives. I have no social conscience. I am a political slug. She has gaiety, vitality, the nurturing power that keeps all life continuing.

Yvonne's quite right, says the cockatiel at my ear.

Shut your beak, you feathered hypocrite, I snarl.

What did you say? asks Yvonne.

Ah, nothing, really. Nothing at all.

That's it O'Donnell, you really have nothing to say, yells Yvonne.

The cockatiel begins a slow dance, begins to whistle, so long, it's been good to know you.

Shut up! I yell at the bird.

It's not the bird that's the problem, cries Yvonne.

She's suddenly very angry.

She picks up her coat, the black leather bag, finds the keys to her van and leaves. As the door slams, a cold gust of loss, regret, rushes past me. I look at the bird. It is asleep on its perch already, its head tucked neatly under its left wing. I detect a grin on its face. The little draught of cold air ruffles its feathers lightly, and is gone.

26

I HAVEN'T SEEN YVONNE in nine days. I miss her. Jesus, that's nowhere near it. I'm really lost, damn near desperate. I don't understand how she got herself so deeply into my life. Damn it, that's not true. I know. She's the only human being I've really talked to. And now I need her near me all the time.

A penny for your thoughts, calls the cockatiel.

Ah, nothing, I say.

Fair value I'd say, replies the cockatiel, but let me guess. You wouldn't be thinking about a certain young woman, would you?

None of your business, I shout, too loudly.

Oh. We are upset, chides the cockatiel. Let's see, how long is it? Over a week since she's been here. That's the story. Mooning over love. Poor Romeo. Romeo! Romeo! Wherefore art thou, Romeo?

Ah, shut up, I say sadly.

There's no point in taking it out on me, huffs the bird, it's obviously all your fault.

What do you mean, I cry.

Dear boy, intones the cockatiel, you've had a wonderful sexual encounter. But nothing more. A mere beast with two backs. No meaningful relationship. No depth of exchange emotionally or intellectually. No exchange of soul. Mere flesh. Yes, mere flesh.

Hell, we get on great, I cry, I don't know what's the matter with her.

Precisely my point, preaches the cockatiel, you know absolutely nothing about her and she's realized you don't really care about her, and she's stopped coming to see you.

Bullshit, I say. But it's an automatic reflex. Damn the bird. It's probably right. Anyhow I've got to do something about it. I can't cross her off the list.

Well, what does Chief Wise Feathers suggest? I ask with as much sarcasm as I can muster.

Oh, dear, chortles the cockatiel, such need disguised in so much bitterness. You are a mess. The obvious thing is to go and see the woman. Talk to her. Tell her you want to work out what's wrong between you. Be honest and open. Put it all out there on the table.

But I've never been to her place, I say.

Oh, precisely the point, the cockatiel sighs, shaking its head, precisely the point. Do you know why you haven't been to see her? enquires the cockatiel.

Never had to, I reply.

Oh, no, cries the cockatiel, there's a larger, more disturbing reason. You sir, are in love with Thanatos!

What? The bird is on a rant.

Death, cries the cockatiel, flapping its wings wildly, you have a death wish. You feel guilty because you're still alive and your friends, Wacker, Harris, the others, are all dead. You wish to destroy yourself out of guilt.

No, I protest.

That's why, yells the bird, you reject Yvonne. That's why you're practising self-immolation. You're burying yourself here. Hiding out in a prison.

I don't get it, I say.

Don't be stupid, screams the cockatiel, that woman is your chance at life. She is Eros. Love. Life. But you prefer death. You prefer to curl up in a hidden grave. All those excuses about them finding you are sheer nonsense. You're afraid of life. Of getting out into the world. So you hide like a scared rabbit. You'd rather be dead. Thanatos is your lover! The bird leans forward and screams, Thanatos! Thanatos! I'm freaked out. Its face is that of a beaked horrible monster. Finally, it flies off. I'm shell-shocked for a couple of minutes. Is the bird right? The very idea is a time bomb that galvanizes me into action.

I pick up a couple of her books to return. It's a transparent excuse, but all I can think of. I walk out into the backyard. The red Ford I bought off Joe Bob in the pub for a hundred bucks leans drunkenly down on the back left side. I brush off the powdered snow. Turn the key. It grunts and snorts into life. Amazing that it goes at all. I only ever use it to go to the pub now and then, or to buy groceries. I stuff a nest of wires back up under the dash. No instruments work. I'm thinking furiously about what to say. I put the address and phone number in her spidery writing on the passenger seat. I've had it for months. As I'm driving I'm trying to work out what went wrong. It's not that tough. I've taken her for granted. It's crazy that this is the first time I've been to see her in her place. Jesus, I'm a dumb bastard. I bang my fist on the dash in anger at myself. Shit. The gas gauge and the speedo start to work. I start laughing. A bit crazily.

It's an apartment building. Four storeys, all jammed one on top of the other. Little pellets of snow or hail begin to fall. I press the buzzer in the entrance.

Yes? Yvonne's voice.

It's me. Jack.

What do you want? Her voice is cold enough to freeze the balls off a brass monkey.

I've got to talk to you, I say.

What about? Another blast from the South Pole.

Yvonne, let me in. I've got to see you.

Why?

I want to work out what's wrong. With us.

Silence. An electric buzz. The latch clicks. The apartment door is open. Hell, the cockatiel is right. That's the open sesame phrase all right. But now I'm on my own. I walk upstairs, down a corridor, counting numbers. Boy, this is anonymous territory. Every door's the same. I find 302. Knock.

Come in, says Yvonne in a most disinterested voice. I follow her through the door. It's a tiny apartment, or at least it looks tiny because it's overflowing with furniture. Big stuffed leather armchairs and a sofa. Chairs stacked six high. A big dining table jammed up against a wall. Books piled up in rows everywhere. You can hardly walk about. A tiny little kitchen with two fridges. It's as if a whole house full of stuff is crammed into one tiny room. A whole raft of paintings and prints is stacked up in one corner. It's like no one is really settled in to live here. Not really unpacked. It's all temporary. Ready for a quick flit somewhere. I'm puzzled. I wave my arm in the direction of the furniture.

You've got a lot of stuff here, I say pointlessly. I put the books on a table. She ignores me. Sits down. I stand there awkwardly.

Yvonne, I drag it out somehow, I need to talk to you. She looks at me for a bit. Gets up, goes to one of the sideboards, gets a cigarette, lights it, takes a little puff. I didn't know you smoked, I say lamely.

Just add it to the list, O'Donnell, she says dryly, you don't know much about me at all, do you? And you haven't tried very hard to find out. Oh, yes, it's my fault, too. I've been quite happy with the fun in bed. Ready to slide along like you. Jump on for the ride. Avoid everything like you. Push it under. Hide things about me, like you do.

I need you, Yvonne, I say.

She turns away, puffs. Cigarette smoke hangs in a heavy, still cloud about her. Nothing moves for a few seconds. I don't know what to say. She turns to me again, very prim and proper, knees together, back straight, all business.

If, she says, you need someone, and if you need me, what's in it for me? Specifically, O'Donnell, for this person here, sitting across from you, who, you say, you need. What's in it for me?

It's a tough question. To answer honestly. I struggle for a decent answer. Try not to bullshit. To find a real answer. And everything I come up with is selfish, what I need. What can I do for Yvonne? She sees me struggling.

What's the problem, O'Donnell?

Everything I think of is selfish, I say desperately, everything is what I need you for. I can't see a bloody thing you'd really need me for.

That's an honest answer, she says, but not good enough.

Yeah, I say, I see your point. It's just that I'm learning so much from you. The books. The talks we have.

Go to college, O'Donnell, she says disdainfully.

Yeah, yeah, I say, quick, but I miss you.

Buy a poodle, she spits, or go and buy one of those floozies you've had in the past.

I've already got the bird, I say, I need someone to share things with.

Huh, she says contemptuously. She's about ready to put the boot in. I feel like a big abyss is opening up. But I'm not going down without a struggle.

Look, I say, surprised at how firm my voice is. You can sit there and look down on me. I deserve it. I've taken you for granted. Thought only of myself. I haven't bothered to really get to know you. But listen love, I'm as straight as I know how with you. I came here because I care about you. I admire your brains and your courage and your ideals even if I tease you about them. And I think about you all the time and I care how you feel. I reckon I should try a lot harder to understand you. But you've just let me talk, mostly, and you haven't talked about yourself . . .

You won't listen, she interrupts dispassionately. I hate it when she's cold and clinical.

I try to listen, I say.

I'm faltering. There's a horrible silence. She sits back and takes a hefty drag of smoke.

Images of past scenes flit past me. Then I see something. The tai chi fight. The way she curled into a ball afterwards. Her nervous laugh. Her horror at killing the salmon. The way, sometimes, I feel she's scared I'll hurt her when we make love. Like she's too scared to let go. I get a flash. A bit of an insight. It's a gamble. I feel the penny in my pocket. It's tails. Have a go, you mug.

I lean forward to touch her. She pulls back. Yvonne, I say, don't run away. Tell me. Has someone, sometime, tried to hurt you? Has some bloke given you a hard time?

What! she cries. She's startled. Totally surprised.

Some man, I pursue, blindly, some lover, did he hurt you? Somehow? I trail off. She leaps to her feet. Jams the cigarette in the ash tray. Glares at me.

Bull's-eye, I think.

Get out of here, O'Donnell, she cries.

No, I say firmly, I'm not going to run away. Who hurt you?

She storms about the room, picks up a cup, dumps it in the sink, flings two magazines in the garbage. I feel like I'm in the eye of a storm. I know if I move, if I go, I'll never see her again. I've hit the mark by sheer bloody luck. I have to know now. I have to get her to tell me, wait it out, tough it out, till it all spills out. Finally, she collapses on the couch, curls up in a ball and rocks like a little kid. She's so vulnerable. I go over to her, but I don't touch her.

Tell me, I say, maybe I can help you. I want to know. What happened?

She calms down a bit. Talks in a flat dispassionate voice.

I've lied to you, O'Donnell. If that's your name.

Yes, I say, I'm really Jack O'Donnell. And I'm really here. And I really want to know.

She rocks a bit. This is going to be painful. Maybe I should get the hell out of here. Avoid trouble. Take off. Leave this mess all behind. But I can't.

I've never had a black man, or any other lovers, she says. Her voice is quiet and cool. You're the second man I've slept with, O'Donnell. The first was my husband. I'm still married.

You're married! I'm totally shaken.

Separated, she says. Married for another year. Then I'll get divorced. I left him. In Toronto. We had a house on Markham Street. Very fashionable. That's why all this furniture is jammed in here. She waves her arm at the overflowing apartment.

Why, I prompt, why did you leave him?

You want to know it all, O'Donnell? All the sick stupidity of it?

Yes, I say quietly, yes, I do.

She sits up and looks at me. I cannot stand how bitterly sad her face is. I can't take her suffering. I reach out to touch her, but she pushes my hand away.

Well, O'Donnell, she cries, the bastard beat me. Yes. He beat me.

She's reacting to the disbelief in my face.

I'm a classic case. Married halfway through university. Starry eyed. He was a young lawyer. The first time was during an argument, a couple of slaps. Not much. I thought it was my fault. I was ashamed. Then he'd pick on things I'd do or say in public. He'd rant and rave at me afterwards. If I yelled back he'd slap me. I felt guilty, ashamed, thought it was my fault. I was disappearing as a person. Tried to change, to fit in. I felt like I was in prison for two years. Then I ran away. He caught me the first time. Beat me badly. Then I ran all the way out here.

I shake my head in disbelief. Someone, anyone, beating

Yvonne. No. I put my head down, feel like crying. She stands up. Walks away.

You're disgusted, O'Donnell, aren't you?

No, I say, just amazed. And upset. I didn't know. I didn't suspect. That was what you were trying to tell me, wasn't it. That's when we had that fight over the tai chi: Why you hate fishing, why you work at the Crisis Centre?

I sit there looking at my hands. They seem gross and mis-shapen, somehow. Like bits of twisted driftwood you see on the beach, gnarled and worn. It occurs to me that Yvonne and I are both refugees, swung in by some strange tide onto this island. Bits of flotsam tossed into a tangle together.

I think you'd better go now, Jack, she says.

I don't want to, I say.

I have to think, Jack, she says, I have to work things out. I'm glad you came. But leave me alone for a while. I'll phone you.

I get up, go over to her, try to hold her. She turns away.

No, Jack. Just leave me alone. Seriously.

She's adamant. Closed up. I don't even protest. I walk past her, pick my way through the apartment out into the cold.

27

I ENDED UP in a Yank hospital in Da Nang. I'd stumbled out of the jungle onto a road two days after I'd got away. Some Yanks driving supply trucks found me staggering down the highway, raving nuts with fever and septic feet.

After I'd calmed down I told them the story.

They sent a couple of choppers out looking for Wacker. They found him, dead, washed up downstream a bit. I went into a bit of a fit about that, apparently. Took a couple of them to hold me down while they shot me full of morphine. Later they told me he was pretty shot up. There were half a dozen NVA bodies there too. They had his papers and stuff. Someone was going to bring them in to me. I never saw them.

Great place that Yank hospital. Fed like a bloody king. Steaks, fries, ice cream, even a canteen with beer when I could move about a bit later on. The nurses were pretty lively, interested in someone not from the States. Ignorant, though, the lot of them. Didn't even know we were in the war. Knew bugger all about Australia, too. One was a freckled redhead named Jessie, bony and hard with a harsh New York twang. I lied to her the most. Tried to get her into bed with me. I was in love with her bony elegant nose. I told her enough Aussie snake and shark stories to keep her excited, though. Reinforce the myth. A bit of bullshit. Women love it.

I was happy as Larry in there. You wouldn't have winkled me out with a pig sticker. Until these Yank intelligence blokes started turning up. There were two of them. Fat and Skinny, I called them. They wanted to know a hell of a lot. At first it was about my capture and escape. Just straight stuff. No, I didn't have a clue how they got our number in the ambush we set for them that turned out to be our ambush. Stupid questions.

No, I didn't know why they held Wacker and me. No clue about what happened to the other blokes. No. More nos. A couple of yesses. We had been at the bridge where the two Yanks had been executed. Yes, the black car. Not a clue about what happened there or why. No, I hadn't picked up anything lying around. Of course Wacker and I'd been puzzling that one out for weeks. Why shoot two civilians in the head? Didn't look right. It still bothered us. But I didn't tell these bastards. No, I hadn't picked up anything lying around.

The old guy was easier. He was chubby and sweated long rivulets down his red face. He reckoned I was dumb. Just dumb and lucky I survived. The other one was tall and baby faced, light blond eyebrows. Blue eyes. He was suspicious. I recognized him. He'd been at the bridge. I can see his face now. The innocence a mask for all kinds of horrors.

How come you left your buddy there to die? he asked. That got to me. I told them about Wacker's feet, how he looked at me, told me to piss off, how I knew he didn't have a chance. But I felt then, as I do now, that I should have stayed. Maybe we both might have got away. Maybe we'd both be dead. But, survival. Rule number one. After that, no rules. I admitted to them that maybe I should have stayed. But I know deep down Wacker wanted me to go, that somehow he knew his luck was gone, that he'd stepped over the edge out of the gambling circle and no spinning penny was going to land the right way up for him. I'll never know for sure.

They kept coming back to something missing at the bridge. Not money. I got the feeling there was the tip of an iceberg in that scene. That those two Yanks with their heads blown off, slumped with their hands tied behind their backs, had been into some big scam. Dope peddling, black market, buying intelligence. Who knows? I'll never know. It's a known fact that everything gets more crooked as you work your way to the top, and that the stink's worse under the roof of a pigsty. So those two Yanks were crooked and got caught. So what difference did it make in this totally bloody insane war where bodies were blowing apart in the hundreds every day?

But the buggers kept coming back. Finally, I said, Look, I can't bloody help you if I don't know what you're on about.

The older one took off his hat. He had a rim of white flesh all about his bald dome. Like a halo. Hello, I thought, this bastard's an angel.

We're investigating the possible murder of those civilians, the old bloke said.

I laughed. Kept on laughing. Here in the middle of a bloody war where there were more shattered bodies, more blood and coiled worm intestines spattered everywhere or burnt to a black stinking crisp every day, here these two jokers were talking about a couple of murders. I laughed till I was damn near crying. It was Monty Python, the whole bloody war. You're talking to someone and bingo, his head shatters, talk a bit more, bingo, his arm disintegrates, another question, bingo, his legs fall off, and the torso does a slow comic tumble sideways. How could you take it seriously? Were we knights in white armour on a holy crusade? Murder? Here in Vietnam? So that was it. Someone had murdered those two Yanks. They looked at me laughing, and got up. He's crazy, the old one said. Like a fox, said Baby Face.

Why? Why had they made the two Americans kneel down with their hands tied behind their backs and shot them in the back of the head? I'd thought they were women for a second, their hair was so long. But they were men all right. There'd been no struggle, no signs of a fight. The two Yanks had walked into some meeting they'd arranged, probably unarmed, and been executed. It was some kind of official meeting, too, because of the car. Not an ambush; the black Mercedes was parked carefully, no skid marks, no bullet holes.

And taking their stuff. It was normal for over there. Different rules. It wasn't like robbing the dead. You saw a body, you went through its pockets, took what was there, automatically. Usually there was just junk. A few bits of paper money, a cheap watch, photos. The corpse had no use for things of the living any more.

When I stopped laughing I began to cry.

Jessie brought me a shot of morphine.

Don't laugh at your own jokes, buddy, she said. It'll make you crazy.

No one understood that the whole of the world was falling apart, that there was no centre and bits were falling off. Like a Disney cartoon I was one of those animals buzz-sawed into slices, hammered flat as dough, squeezed into toothpaste, collapsing from within.

I started to tell Jessie. But she didn't listen. She only liked me when I was funny. She faded away.

I slept.

28

A CRASH in the middle of the night brings me running into the living room. The cage is down on the ground and the cockatiel lies stunned on the gravel paper at the bottom. I examine the hook. Somehow it has been spun out of the ceiling. How? I give the cockatiel a sip of Courvoisier.

My God, gasps the bird, that was a shock. I got the cage circling really fast, and I practised flying under and over the perches. That's how they trained gladiators in Rome. Under and over. Up and down. You know. Keeps your reaction time right up there. Especially in the dark. Next thing I know the cosmos is at the Big Bang stage again!

I put the cage up, screw the hook in tight, put the cover over the bird.

Sweet dreams, I say, but the bird is already asleep.

I sit down, and for the tenth time, try to write a letter to Yvonne, and for the tenth time, tear it up. And for the tenth time I think of packing up and pissing off, somewhere, anywhere. But I can't. Then I think, O'Donnell, you dumb bastard, are you going to walk away without a fight, let her go that easily? And I get angry, and pull a sheet of paper over and write:

> Yvonne, my love, You're the first woman and the only woman I've ever loved. If I've made a mess of it, it's because I'm still learning the rules. I didn't listen to you, but I will. As you say, I'm full of anger and outrage. But those

scars will heal in time and so, I think, will yours. I hope we can have a chance to help each other. I'd like to ask you to start over. May I invite you to my place for a cup of tea.

Yours Truly
Jack O'Donnell.

I read it over. It's pathetic. But I post it anyhow.

29

YOU'D THINK I WAS TRYING to write deathless bloody verse the way the cockatiel carries on. Hell, I'm just trying to get a few bits and pieces down as they happened or, at any rate, as I saw them happen—that's the best you can do, I reckon. I've got to work it out of my system. But the bird keeps carrying on about flawed perception and the inbuilt inaccuracy of language. Can't even take a joke, the feathered freak. I told it the one about the Irishman who emigrated to Australia, thereby raising the IQ level in both countries, and the damn bird just nodded its head. Not even a giggle. It was the same when I made a joke yesterday about Yvonne being a Martian because she didn't understand Australian men. God, I miss that woman.

The cockatiel raised its left claw and scratched its left wattle very slowly.

That's very interesting, the bird said reflectively, I have heard women on several occasions speculate about their place on this planet. They suggest that there really may not be a proper niche for them, that they may indeed be foreigners or aliens from another planet.

Don't be stupid, I laugh.

But the cockatiel is serious. He's put on his English don voice.

It is possible, says the bird. Consider those strange markings on the land in South America. Von Daniken is it, who mentions them? Yes, perhaps the aliens, in a philanthropic coup, worked a very clever genetic engineering process to make human reproduction dependent upon women, thus ensuring after many generations that they would rise to power, thus eliminating the crude, savage, and violent habits of the original bisexual male inhabitants. Yes, cries the cockatiel, that would explain why the only hair women can stand is on their own heads. Certainly they go through all kinds of excruciating exercises to rid themselves of the other hair. Probably, on another planet, they were hairless. Ahah. And that's why they are so unhappy with their bodies. Always complaining that they're too big here or too small there. That's it. A vestigial body memory forces them to deprive and push and shove their bodies into other shapes. And of course . . . Here, the cockatiel slaps his head highly with one claw . . . that would explain make-up. The vestigial memory of face.

Vestigial what? I exclaim.

Ah yes, dear boy, a memory trace, a fragmentary and imperfect recollection of what their alien appearance may have been on another planet. This may explain their constant efforts with paint and powder to recreate another visage. This is most fascinating. There is no doubt about their entirely different emotional make-up. Probably a glitch in the alien computer that originally designed them. Attempting to create a form which would fit into earthlings, it substituted a totally different emotional make-up. Probably couldn't conceive of the low form of earth mind it was endeavouring to duplicate. That's why they have this third eye, this inner perception we crudely label intuition, which is not readily perceived in the older more primitive brain of men. Thus their sexuality is more holistic than the dinosaur drive of males like yourself. And naturally, their sense of order and harmony is more refined than males', particularly on a social level, coming originally as they do from a more advanced planet. Yes, that's why such primitive entertainments as hunting and fishing rarely engage the Martians' full attention. And it would follow that crude battles of a physical kind are well below their level of development. That's why, you poor dear boy, Yvonne, that woman you used to know, avoids watching those horrendous bone-crunching and primitive sports on TV. Football, hockey, boxing—all exist at a substandard level of evolved life form.

There's a lot of skill involved in sport, I protest.

But surely you must only feel pain and deep sympathy when you see the hulking wretches stumble and stutter unintelligibly on TV when they're interviewed. Mere brute force and ignorance must be replaced with a higher form of language and intuition. Yes, I think I'm really onto something here, mumbles the cockatiel, where is my notebook? Meet it is that I set it down.

30

I WAS JUST FINISHING my hospital breakfast when he walked in. Every morning, eggs and bacon, toast and marmalade. Great tucker here in Yank heaven.

G'day mate, he said and flopped into the chair next to my bed. Jesus, I've gotta thirst that'd make a camel weep. He was about thirty, I reckon, splotchy face from booze, long dark hair, short beard, red-rimmed bloodshot brown eyes. He looked utterly shagged, hungover, dissolute. A Pentax swung sideways about his neck.

Gerry's the name, he held out his hand, I'm an ink-stained wretch from ABC. Supposed to turn you into a fucking hero. Noble exploits of the lad from Down Under and all that shit.

I dunno, I said, I'm no hero.

Ha! he said. You wait. Can you walk? he asked. Let's have a heart starter at that bar across the road. No one was around. I threw on my gear.

It was a pretty low dive, with posters of Hollywood movie stars everywhere. Bogart. Marilyn Monroe. Old stuff. Dark bamboo walls and ceiling, two lazy fans, three bored and plain Vietnamese bargirls who gave up on us pretty quick.

So, said Gerry, gulping down a beer and making a long face, let's get the story shit out of the road so we can have a serious drink. I've got your name and all that official American background bulldust. What really happened?

I'm no hero, I said, tipping up the beer, I left my mate behind.

Yeah? he was only mildly interested. Why?

His feet were stuffed, I said. I tried to carry him. But he stopped me. He was hurting like hell. I thought he might shoot me.

That's a good reason. Gerry wrote quickly as I told him the story. He took some photos, wrote down what I said.

Yeah, he said. I can make something of that. All you have to do is keep out of trouble till the election next week and you can walk off the plane in Australia a first-class hero.

What election? I asked.

He looked surprised. The Aussie election, you dumb shit. Whitlam's gonna win and pull all of you arseholes out of here.

Ah, I said, you can't trust politicians.

Gerry looked at me as if I was a cretin. He stroked his beard. He was deciding something.

Who would you vote for? he asked, very quietly.

Probably the DLP, I said. Someone who's anticommunist.

What! says Gerry, they're the crazy bastards who got you here getting shot at in the first place!

That began my intensive drunken political education. I've never forgotten it. He started with Archbishop Mannix and the groupers, right-wing Catholics secretly taking over the unions in Australia, fighting communism with God. How the church got deeply into politics and gained a lot of power through the DLP. How they used the same tactics as the commies. Jesus, I thought that was crooked. Priests in politics! Gerry reckoned B. A. Santamania was behind it all, using the DLP to throw up a commie scare that buggered up the ALP. This way he mixed up religion and politics so no one knew the difference.

How'd you like the Pope as your prime minister? Gerry asked sarcastically.

I thought a bit.

No. That wouldn't work. I see your point, I said, and Gerry went on about the pressure the DLP had put on against anything left wing. This ended up making it easier for Aussie to send troops to Vietnam, advisers first, then more and more troops, until they had to bring in the Birthday Bullet. It didn't make sense. Vietnam was so far away. We were on the wrong horse there. Yeah, I said, but the Vietnamese asked us to help. Who, asked Gerry, those poor bloody peasants whose villages you burn down?

I dunno, I said, I suppose it's the bigwigs again. Anyway what about democracy? I asked.

Gerry shook his head. He told me about the vote to join North and South Vietnam. I'd never heard of it. How Diem buggered it up so he could run the whole South Vietnamese show as kingpin. Yeah, but Ho Chi Minh's a dictator, I cried. He probably is now, Gerry said, but he started off as a nationalist. He just wanted to liberate Vietnam. He begged the Yanks years ago to help free Vietnam from the French. The Yanks ignored him.

No, I answered, that can't be right.

Look, Gerry said quietly, you don't know fuck all, so why don't you just shut up and listen.

So I did. I heard about the bullshit in the Gulf of Tonkin, how the U.S. government blew the incident up, exaggerated a couple of torpedo boats into a threat of major conflict and grabbed the chance to widen the whole bloody war. How the Aussie papers parroted the Yanks. Gerry had had his stories edited or ignored lots of times.

How do you know all this? I demanded.

Reading, Gerry replied, ever heard of it? Books, magazines, newspapers.

Well, that got to me. Were we so stupid, Harris, Wacker, the lot of us, that we'd put our lives on the line for bullshit; that we didn't even have a clue about how we were being used? I made up my mind there and then that if I ever got out of this mess of a war, I'd get some of the books Gerry talked about and try to get a hold on what made the world go round.

A bargirl, short dark hair, purple eyeshadow, blood-red lips, came up to us, gave us a little smile from her round face, swung her hips in her miniskirt.

You want boom-boom? she said. Her hand went quick as a tiger snake down into Gerry's trousers.

No sweetheart, not before breakfast, Gerry said. She squirmed her hand about.

I boom-boom you long time. Long long time, she said.

Bugger off, love, Gerry said gently.

Faggy fag, spat the bargirl and swirled away.

Do you think that girl is interested in democracy? Gerry asked.

No. I laughed. Most of the Vietnamese just wanted to grow

their rice and pigs and get on with it. They couldn't give a damn about politics. All they saw was armed men taking their possessions and killing their sons. It was a crazy, depressing mess. How the hell did Aussie get into this? I demanded. The Yanks made some veiled threats, Gerry said, told the Aussie government they'd pull out investments, hinted that they'd drop the protective umbrella around Australia so we'd be fair game for anyone who wanted to move in.

Nah, I cried, Aussie could protect itself.

Don't be naive, Gerry replied, with three ships and ten planes and a couple of thousand of you poor footslogging buggers? Forget it.

Oh, he said, I forgot the CIA. They had people working down in Australia to get up the good old slant-eyed commie fear. The DLP loved it. Aussie is still paranoid about the Japanese from World War II. Scares the daylights out of Australians, the idea of some Asians invading. So that made it easier for people to accept sending troops to Vietnam. We could be the next domino, that kind of crap. It all worked. Now we've got this huge secret bloody police down there. Ever heard of the Australian Security and Information Offices?

No, I said. I found all of this hard to believe.

Before Vietnam, Australia only had a dozen or so pensioners in hotel doormen's uniforms grabbing the odd Russian spy off the plane in Darwin, Gerry said, now it's a massive spiderweb spread through the whole country, fostered and trained by the Yank CIA.

Go on, I protested, Aussies wouldn't stand for it.

They're like you, Gerry said, dumber than a hundred head of sheep. They wouldn't have a clue.

Jesus, I was getting drunk and pissed off. There were all these dark forces out there running things, and particularly running me.

I had another go at Gerry.

Yeah, but how do I know you're not bullshitting me?

Gerry did his nut. He bellowed his anger at my ignorance.

I bellowed back my anger and disbelief.

At five o'clock, he was still at it. I was damn near weeping. By six that night I was suffering from alcoholic remorse and over-information. Drunkenly, I told him about the two civilians, the black Mercedes, the Yank MPs questioning me. He was instantly alert. He was one of those bastards that booze doesn't seem to change. I was utterly sad, desperate at the thought that I'd been killing people for the wrong cause. Sucked in, bullshitted to, whisked like a bit of dry cowshit into some crazy vortex I didn't understand.

Gerry went off to make some phone calls.

At 6:30 Jessie came into the bar with two orderlies, and I was unceremoniously dragged out and down the street back to the hospital. The next day, everybody was very, very cool.

The doctor sniffed, the nurses walked by with withering looks. I was so brutally hungover I didn't care. And guilt is for girls, as Wacker always said.

You'd think they'd be used to someone having a few beers. But they couldn't handle the flip side of the Aussie character; the fun had turned a bit sour, the uniqueness had worn off, and trouble had emerged grinning out of the piss tank. I was used to it. I slept most of the day.

31

I'VE BEEN READING a hell of a lot lately, writing as well, trying to forget Yvonne. I don't want to end up like one of those ball-less blokes back in Aussie, who end up tagging along behind their wives, wheeling the kid in a pram behind Mum, while she's out front, brassy and loud, barging through the world, only turning around to take a swipe at her piss-weak hubby. You know those blokes who hand over their whole weekly pay cheque to Mum, and then get back five bucks to have a beer. Yvonne's strong enough to take over. But I'm not going to end up like that. To hell with women.

I've been on my Pat Malone all my life and done pretty well. Why change? I'd have to give up too much doing what I want to do when I want to do it, with whomever I want to. I can still chase the stray and exotic pieces of fluff who pop up here and there. The ability to pick up and go whenever and wherever I want to. I'd lose all that. Bugger it, I'm not going to be tied down. Yvonne can stay away forever. I'll be okay. I'll survive.

The cockatiel flies over, reads this last piece, and cackles sardonically.

Dear boy, the bird observes, patronizingly, you are hooked. Yvonne really has you where she wants you.

No bloody way, I snarl, she's not getting to me.

Methinks the lad doth protest too much, observes the cockatiel and flits off to its perch.

That's it, I decide, I need a break. I'm going fishing.

Do take care, calls the bird as I walk to the front door, carrying oars, life jacket, and rods. The sea is quite unforgiving.

Actually, the sea is platinum calm. I row easily out toward the five islets near the Winchelseas. A Voodoo jet rumbles overhead. They must be playing at war out beyond the islands in Whiskey Gulf. Sure enough, there's the dark outline of a submarine cruising out past Grey Rock. It's ironic, these machines of war here, where everything about me for 360 degrees is pure calm splendour: The silver sea, the low violet outlines of the islands, the dark blue shores of this island and the mainland, and above them the purple mountains topped with stunning white snow peaks. You couldn't paint it or photograph it with any truth. And in the midst of it you feel tiny and pointless, except that you're warm and breathing and seeing, and all of that out there, surrounding you, is cold and inanimate and blind. And somehow you feel more important because you can move in the midst of it, can observe its changing shapes and colours, and in this way participate in it.

I put two large cut herring over the side, attach two twelve-ounce weights, and row slowly. The third islet comes nearer, a greyish-white island, fifty yards around, covered in sea gull shit, and at this time of the year dotted with the blubbery and raucous shapes of sea lions and seals here to feed on the swarming mass of herring waiting to spawn in the bay. The stench of the islet is horrible—that sickly bacterial fleshy decay I've smelt in Vietnam.

I'm about a hundred yards off, rowing slowly, no strikes, when I see the killer whales—eighteen or twenty feet of black muscle, with white moon markings and high fins, working in a pod a mile off, rolling up to breathe, then disappearing under the sea while another two or three surge up and down again.

All the dark shapes on the islet galvanize into action as the killer whales approach. Some lumber into the sea and disappear. The bulk of them jackknife and waddle, snorting and grunting up to the safety of the high point of the islet. I turn the boat around. They tell me orcas have never taken a human, but I don't want to set any records. Besides, I know sharks in Aussie, and how erratically they behave.

Two young seals obviously haven't got the message. They're playing tag with each other at the water's edge, gambolling happily like puppies. A hundred yards off, the orcas disappear. I yell out to the seal pups, innocent and oblivious to the danger, but that's false human sympathy, useless.

In a great burst of spray, a huge explosion out of the water, one great orca erupts, half its length, huge mouth open, studded with teeth, chomps down on the struggling seal, and with powerful twists of its body, disappears back into the sea. The second seal is stunned, begins to backpedal, and womph; in a spout of water a second orca blasts out of the sea and takes the other squirming seal.

I pull the rods in. Everything alive here—seals, sea lions, salmon—is quivering in fright, shocked at the sudden eruption of violence. I know the salmon will hide in kelp beds for hours, feeding the last thing on their minds. Pointless to fish. It occurs to me that the bird is right. The whole fucking world is full of violence. You can't avoid it. You've got to live and love with it swirling all about you. Life's just a two-up game. Spin the bloody penny. Heads and tails, love and hate, war and peace, life and death. Yvonne and I have to stop hiding out. You've got to go on regardless. I put the oars out, and row slowly home.

32

JESSIE TAPS ME AWAKE.

There's an Australian doctor here to see you, she says.

Christ, in walks Gerry the Journo, half-full as usual, but in a white coat with a black bag. What a bullshitter. He's told them he's a medico.

Thanks, nurse, he says to Jessie.

You're welcome, doctor, she says and pads off.

I'm snorting with suppressed laughter. Gerry rolls two of the screens around my bed, sits down, opens the black bag, and there's the golden lager of Dr. Foster inside.

Doctor's orders, he says and hands me a can.

What the fuck are you doing here? I ask. You're going to get me in real deep.

No worries, sport, says Gerry. I was interested in that little story you told me about the two Yanks who got executed.

Jesus, I groan. I told you that?

As well as revealing your abysmal ignorance of pretty well every political, economic, and social issue involved in this conflict, Gerry says very properly. But I think you've stumbled, and that's a most accurate word for your capacities, stumbled on something quite sick, even for this sicker than sick war.

What? Gerry's patronizing is beginning to piss me off. So I don't understand it all. Who the hell does? I know damn well I'm just another faceless idiot with a gun, an anonymous body running and shooting in jungle gear at other faceless idiots shooting at me in the same camouflage. But who ran the whole thing, and why, was beyond me. All I understood was the ducking and weaving and side-stepping that kept a man out of trouble. I was good at that. And I smelled trouble now, with Gerry, with the story.

He took a long gobble of beer. Ah, he said, that's a floater.

I was talking to one of the CBS blokes last night. Now listen. It seems that two young Yanks were killed over here about a month ago. Civilians. That'd be about right as far as the time goes. One of them was a senator's son, from California; the other was a reporter for one of these radical little magazines. Somehow, they managed to get credentials, visas and so on, probably through the senator. No one knows exactly what they were up to. Everybody thought they were just doing a story. You know, sad woes of a wartime country. But there's a chance, or a strong possibility, that they were carrying letters or something from some pretty important people in the U.S. and they wanted to set up some sort of independent peace initiative with the Vietnamese. Some kind of people's peace, so I'm told, between the people of the U.S. and the ordinary villagers here in Vietnam. It seems they had a hookup with North Vietnam somehow, through some of the other Yanks who'd already visited Hanoi.

Sounds pretty far-fetched to me, I said.

Not really, Gerry mused. You think about what'd happen in the U.S., to the government and the Pentagon, if these two turned up in San Francisco with a signed peace agreement between some high-ranking VC and North Vietnamese and some Yank senators, movie stars, rock stars, writers and so on. Jesus, it'd cut the government off at its knees. They'd have to follow it up. It'd be a major embarrassment, politically. There's so many people there opposed to the war anyhow. All the hawks'd lose their feathers. It'd be tremendous propaganda for peace. It's a brilliant idea.

Ah, you're exaggerating, I said. Nothing'll stop this fucking war. Besides, the VC killed 'em. They don't want peace. They want us out of the country.

Hah, said Gerry quietly, that's where it gets really ugly, really dirty. What if the VC didn't kill them? What if the CIA or one of those assassination squads from the Green Berets did it? What if those two young men were killed by Americans to prevent them from meeting the VC and signing the documents?

Sounds like a movie to me, I laughed. But I thought about it for a second and that was possible, yeah, that could be just the way it happened. Shoot 'em and leave 'em and they become anonymous, just bits of dead meat to file away and disappear. A cloud of official bulldust and whatever they wanted to do, whoever they were, just disappears. I felt sick. It came home to me that Wacker might've suspected something like that. But I was too dumb.

But why in the Aussie sector, I asked, why not in some Yank area, or in Saigon?

Oh, Gerry shrugged, neutral ground, maybe less suspicious. There's this rumour that the VC can do a lot better against the Yanks than you blokes, so your area's pretty quiet. Just the right place.

Okay, I said, taking another beer out of the black bag. But this is all Disneyland. You've got no proof. You don't know for sure.

Yeah, said Gerry, it's conjecture, it's supposition, it requires corroboration.

Yeah, that's what I meant, I added eagerly at the words of wonder he'd produced. I was jealous. I wished I could talk like that. I was all brawn and no brains. It was embarrassing. I made another silent vow to read like a bastard when I got out of here.

That's where you come in, Gerry said, draining his beer. He pulled out a photo cut out from a newspaper. There were two blokes, waving peace signs at the camera. A Pan Am Boeing 707 stood in the background.

Do you recognize them? he said urgently. It's important.

I looked again. Their faces were so alive, smiling and vital. What I'd seen was blood smeared, muddy, and dead. Yeah, there was something. I remembered the granny glasses. Hippy hair. The long nose. But they could be anyone. Ah, hell, if I said I recognized them the whole business'd explode. I wasn't that dumb. I knew I'd be in trouble. There'd be a million questions. Officers. MPs. The whole bloody lot. All I wanted to do was to get the fuck out of here, out of this hospital, this jungle, this rot and stink of a country.

Even Ceduna looked great right now.

I dunno, I said to Gerry.

You do, you bastard, snarled Gerry, thrusting the photo closer. Take another gander.

Their heads were blown apart, I said. Congealed blood, mud where they'd fallen forward. I can't tell. They could be anybody. I can't tell.

I think you're lying, Gerry hissed.

Suit yourself, I said. Maybe you want it to be true. So it fits your idea of what's happening. Intellectual corruption everywhere. The whole world's sick, eh, Gerry?

I was proud of that little speech. I didn't believe it myself. But it deflated Gerry a lot. Then I felt a bit sorry for him. He'd dug up what was probably the truth. And I was like some desperate mongrel paddling away with my front paws to bury the secret again out of sheer fright, out of sheer self-preservation. He'd have taken them on, the bastards, the bigwigs. Maybe he'd have won, but I knew I didn't have a chance. What did it matter anyhow? My best bet was to look the other way. It was pretty low. Skulking about like a dingo. But that's what I'd learned. Never stick your neck out. Never put your head up above the sandbags. Keep your pecker in your pants. Watch out. Duck. Caution kept you alive.

Gerry packed up the empties. Listen, mate, he said, rather tired, I understand what you're hiding. I'm not going to write you up. Maybe I'm up the creek here. But I don't think so. If you change your mind, get hold of me. Anytime. Okay?

He shambled his way out of the hospital.

I felt like a complete dead loss.

I'd seen two young men killed trying to stop a war, trying to stop me getting killed. And what was my reaction? Chickenshit. I didn't think much of myself.

33

IF YOU WERE A WRITER, concludes the cockatiel, lowering a foolscap page of this story in his left claw, you would know that this is pseudophilosophy disguised as fiction. You have, the bird goes on indignantly, no developed character, no *raison d'être,* no motivation. Furthermore, the piece has no clear structure. No balance. Not even contrapuntal polarity. Frankly, it's not even good enough to put in the bottom of my cage.

What do you expect? I say, I'm just trying to tell the truth. Say what's happening. Record something.

Unfortunately, sneers the cockatiel, for the purposes of traditional fiction that is totally insufficient.

Fuck you, I cry. I'd like to wring the damned bird's neck. It's a know-it-all. A jumped up, supercharged, feathered superego.

Very literate, sneers the bird, very Antipodean, very intelligent and succinct.

34

THEY BRING IN A YANK CASUALTY this morning really early. Young bloke. He ends up on the bed next to me. Chest shot, poor bastard. He's wheezing and squeezing out bubbles of breath. A tiny trickle of bright red bubbles at the corner of his mouth. It looks bad. He looks fifteen, dark crew cut, smooth skin, probably not even shaving yet. It brings out some bitter anger in me. I yell for the nurses to look at the blood in his mouth. He could be drowning in it. The nurses have a look. I know he's gone; they fuss over him, but don't do much really. He's bought the farm. Funny phrase that. We use lots of them to describe death.

He talks to me later, breathless, heaving, tells me he has his papers for R & R in Hong Kong, got shot in the chopper bringing him in to Saigon to catch the plane. Had his dress uniform in a plastic bag with him. Some stray bullet flying up casually into the air from an anonymous hamlet just had to hit him in the chest. The bloke has shithouse luck. I suspect he's a virgin still, straight off some corn farm in Iowa, maybe eighteen, hoping for erotic initiation in Hong Kong. I tell him to relax, he'll get there, just to take it easy. He asks me to get his R & R papers so he can hold them. I find them finally with his dress uniform hanging in a closet. But he's too weak to hold them, so I shove them, signed, sealed, and stamped, under his pillow. Dream on it, mate, I say.

That night he whispers to me. Take them. You go. I'll go another time. Take the papers. You can go. Have one for me in Hong Kong. I look at him. I don't want to pinch his papers. They're his security blanket. But he insists, gets agitated, so I reach for the papers, stuff them away under my pillow. We whisper for a bit. He's got a girl called Donna on the next farm back home. She won't let him touch her. The guys in his outfit tease the hell out of him because he's a virgin. We swap yarns about farming. Jesus, they have farm equipment that'd blow Ceduna's mind. No sheep. A few cattle. He talks about fishing for rainbow trout in a big cold lake. About hunting deer. We drift off to sleep.

He's dead the next morning, wheeled away just as I wake up.

I've had it. It's too much, sitting here safe and watching them die. It's different when you're out there, scrambling about the rice paddies ducking the fire. But this place is artificial, unreal. A farm kid who dies before he knows a woman. I've got to get out. I can still hear the kid's voice yarning away. And now he's gone. This is not a war; this is a series of bad scenes, bad jokes. I can't stand seeing another one die. It's speeding up on me like a Chaplin silent movie. Too many contrasts. The quiet sterile hospital, the stink and screaming terror outside. I decide to leave the hospital. They won't know a thing. I've got a nose for disorder. They're not well organized. I pinch the uniform. A Yank one. Some of the more conscious patients cheer me on when they work out what I'm doing. I rig myself up as a Yank in dress uniform. A corporal. Thought a lift in rank'd help. I look in the bathroom mirror. Neat dress uniform. A gaunt, white face but the uniform is so anonymous, no one'd know I wasn't a Yank. And I just walk out. I'm pretty sure none of those wounded Yanks'll say a word.

I'm a rebellious hero to them. Probably they don't care. By the time the Yank army catches up with my outfit, I'll be back in my tent.

I run into a bunch of Yanks in a bar nearby. Two of them are truck drivers waiting to take a load out. I hitch a ride in a truck with a cigar-smoking Yank Italian from Seattle called Lou. We stop to pick up two fifths of Canadian rye at a bar. I pay. It's Lou's favourite drink. We drink and drive, drive and drink. I hear his life story. It keeps changing. He's glad he's here. He misses his wife. He is heroic, a bum, mistreated, a success, a failure. He gets boisterous, sad, happy, maudlin, and finally passes out.

I drive the truck right up to our camp at dawn. Lou wakes up in the passenger seat holding his head in both hands, has no idea where he is, starts getting scared and pissed off. Curses me as I get out, swings the big Ford around and roars off.

There's two new kids on the gate. Straight in from Oz. I've never seen them before. I spin them a yarn. They hesitate, phone in, but there's no one awake there. Typical. We could get wiped out in ten minutes if the VC decided to attack. There's hardly anybody in camp anyhow, these kids tell me, most of them are out on some sweep, some already gone back to Aussie. Jesus, it's criminal. If Gerry's right, there's only a few days before the Aussie election, and they'll all be flying home. Why send them out to take chances? As if anything makes sense. Byzantine.

I walk in. The kids are right. It's deserted. All the stones marking the driveways are freshly whitewashed. Another army insanity. The rows of tents are silent. The flag's not up yet and it ought to be. There's an uneasy silence about the camp, as if they're all dead and gone. Maybe it's a sign for me. Who would I know, anyhow, except some asshole officers, and they never get touched, never get a scratch. Most of my outfit's already gone: Wacker, Little Sam, Harris, Anderson, Double Barrel—all dead. The rest? Who knows?

I find my tent. There's two other blokes' gear hanging up, bits of their past, a photo or two. All my gear has gone. Every last trace of it. It's like I never existed. I dig quickly under my bunk, find the money belt. The money's all there, wads of it, dark green Yank dollars bulging in the nylon pockets. And the one letter. I have the escape hatch in my hand.

No one comes to check up on me. Maybe the kids decided not to say anything, maybe no one cares. The Australian Army has forgotten me. I'm happy.

I sleep for the rest of the day, pinch some of the cans in the tent for tucker. I have become lost in the army. No one knows who I am, or where I am. No one cares. I have, for all they know, died. Or disappeared. The more I think about it, the more the idea appeals to me. They haven't made the connection or they'd have caught up with me in the Saigon hospital. My identity is in a paper shuffle somewhere on a desk, some unanswered question on the bottom of the sheet. Is he dead? Is he captured? I have glimmerings of a disappearing act to rival Houdini's.

I've got them in a perfect situation. I lie back on the bunk and stare at the canvas roof softly rolling with the breeze. If I disappear now, some army clerk somewhere will solve the problem with a quick decisive move of a stamp in his right hand. KIA. MIA. Address Unknown. Return to Sender. What do they know about us getting captured? Probably they reckon Wacker and I were killed too. Instead we survived through the incredible luck that cannoned Anderson's dead body into both of us from the shock of the mortar round. King shit we were. Knocked bloody stupid. Our cowbells clanged by a flying corpse. If they sent out a patrol to find out what happened, that's what they'd conclude. Missing in Action. There were thousands of soldiers floating about in Vietnam, hundreds dying, hundreds going missing. Who could keep tabs on all of them? I am just one more. I could easily, simply, disappear.

If I sling my hook over the wire and disappear, what're the two kids at the guardhouse going to say? They saw a mysterious Aussie dressed in a Yank's uniform who no one knows, who can't be found anywhere? No. This is my chance. I have the Yank R & R papers for Hong Kong. I can bullshit my way onto the plane. Take the money and run. It isn't as if they'd be overjoyed to see me back here anyway. Probably end up on some shit patrol out on point getting an AK 47 round right between the eyes, just as they counted the last ballot in Perth.

35

JUST AFTER DARK I walk away from the war in Vietnam. It is incredibly easy.

Three days later I am in Kowloon, in an alley arcade off the roar of Nathan Street getting fitted out for slacks, sports coats, and suits by Danny the tailor, who fusses about in his tiny store, offering me beer as I look over rolls of cloth and silk. I have become a rich civilian. I have trouble walking down the streets at first. The mob runs at you, like sheep going nowhere. I learn to side-step and thread my way. I've never seen so many people. They're all after money. All chasing it like mad.

The very rich live high above the swarm in their mansions on the hills. The very poor squatters in plastic tents perch on top of the high-rises or sleep on the streets. It's an obvious and sickening social division, clear-cut and final. I visit the stinking sights of Hong Kong, Aberdeen, the Star Ferry, Macau, always with a different sister of one of my bellhops attentively on my arm.

I've sipped tea and danced to thirties' swing with the girls in Tonnochies, surrounded by Al Capone decor. Taken Suzie Wong back to my room for two hundred Hong Kong dollars. I've had a bantam hen pick out a fortune card with my future on it, but I don't believe a word. In Wanchai I've seen the remarkable physical feat of a young Chinese girl drinking a bottle of Coca-Cola with her nether mouth, then carefully replacing the contents without spilling a drop. In a dark club off Lockhart Road I've seen another Chinese woman simultaneously handle three Yank sailors sexually, though all three, despite her best efforts, lost erections before the big event, to the drunken jeers of their buddies. It is all pretty well a downer, sexual bullshit.

I've bent my neck admiring the fading dove of peace on the façade of Saõ Paulo Cathedral in Macau, watched old men playing checkers under the bust of Luis de Camoes, the sixteenth-century poet who apparently never came here. I've walked past the hungry tigers of slot machines in the shabby Hotel Lisboa, dropped a hundred Hong Kong dollars on roulette in the Macau Palace (a bit better place) while some horrible Chinese opera wailed, watched jai alai, and put a ten-dollar bet on a dog called Wedding Bells. The bastard came dead last. I've eaten stuffed king prawns at Aberdeen and roast pigeon at Fat Siu Hau, the House of the Smiling Buddha, and done my little tourist nuts off. But it has been enough to bring tears to a glass eye, as Wacker would say. I have seen the grotesque and gruesome tableaus in Tiger Balm Gardens, fought off swarms of tea towel sellers, Rolex watch sellers, electronic junk pedlars of every kind in Tsim Sha Tsui, and I have retreated finally to the small but dynamic double bed in the Marco Polo.

Wacker would've loved it. I got drunk and weepy a couple of nights thinking about him. I feel like all my emotions have been cut off, pruned at the base. But the girls do wonderful sympathetic massages. I have the Chinese bellhops bowing as they bring in chicken cordon bleu to my hotel room in the Marco Polo, where one of their many sisters, so it seems, sits up in bed each day, coyly, with the sheets held over her small breasts, smiling as I put another twenty Hong Kong dollars as a tip in one of her many brothers' quite capacious hands. One of the girls I ran into, with the unlikely name of Samantha Hong, has got me three passports, all genuine, all fallen off the same truck in Wanchai, for the total price of two thousand U.S. dollars. I now have three different names, three different photos, Australian, Canadian, and American identities. But I am spending too much money here in the stink and lovely sin of Kowloon, where there is a magic refrigerator in my hotel room which mysteriously replenishes itself with booze and food without me noticing, until the horrible prices appear on the Marco Polo bill as I check out after a week of lascivious anonymity. Samantha, surprisingly, turns up at the hotel entrance as I'm being ushered into a Jaguar airport limousine. Has she mistaken commerce for love? No. She kisses me and asks me for money for an abortion. She has squeezed tears into her lovely almond eyes, tells me her future will be ruined. It's biologically impossible in terms of time. She thinks I'm pretty dumb. I shove a wad of Hong Kong money into her sexually adept hands. As the limo pulls out, she has her dark head down rapidly leafing through the bills. She does not even wave good-bye. It is touching. I am suddenly heartily sick of hot countries, raucous shrill voices, and the sight of hands outstretched for money. I have one imitation Gucci suitcase, a number of silk shirts, imitation Dior tailored jackets and strides, etc.—all phony, like Hong Kong. But the real freedom is that I can go anywhere I want.

I deliberately do not tip the limo driver at the airport. He yells some Cantonese obscenity at me. I feel cleaner. Inside the airport, soldiers walk about with machine guns. It could be Saigon. I am sick of Asia, and heat. There must be a clean cool place somewhere.

The next plane leaving is Pan Am to San Francisco and Vancouver, British Columbia, in Canada. It sounds cold and western, peaceful and quiet. I buy a one-way ticket. The headline on the *Sydney Herald* as I walk through the international newsstand says, "Whitlam Victory." I buy a *Playboy* magazine and book in for my flight.

36

I AM SICK OF THIS BIRD—its arrogance, its pontifications, its huge ego that swells within the house, its pretensions, its selfishness, its decadence, its strange sexuality, its lack of civility, generosity of spirit, and warmth. I must even hide what I'm writing right now for fear of critical evaluation. This is how the Ancient Mariner must have felt when the dead albatross was hung about his neck. But what can one do with a pet who grows to such gargantuan proportions in one's consciousness. Strangle the bloody thing? Starve it to death? Take it back to the pet shop and risk public exposure from its bizarre and unique talents? I mean, would the cockatiel lapse into silence? Hell no. It would lambast and belabour and lie scurrilously about its treatment so that I would emerge as a pariah. An unfeeling beast who mistreats innocent birds. I can visualize the scene. TV cameras, reporters, crowding as the bird sobs and tearfully compares me to an S.S. monster in Auschwitz. The public outcry would bury me. Let it go? Now, that's a thought that keeps circling like a hawk in my mind. A simple slip. Forget the door is open; the cockatiel tries one little experimental outing into the open air. Slam the door shut. No. The bird damn near knows what I'm thinking most of the time. Besides, it is openly opposed to the concept of wild kingdom whenever I suggest it. Give the bird to Yvonne? The bird, I'm sure, would love to have her on his own for whatever perverse reasons run in its tiny feathered head. Damn thing tried to toss me heads or tails for her last week. Faint hope.

And would I be happy with that? Wouldn't the thought of the bird manipulating Yvonne into God knows what situation cause me more anxiety than I have now? Damn it. I'm stuck with the cursed thing. Blessed with the damned. Yoked with a mind from many pasts. And cockatiels, I read, live to be twenty years or older. Hell and brimstone, in a court of law that's a life sentence. What have I done to deserve this? Can't I just ship the son of a feathered bitch straight back to Alice Springs. Why me? Why me?

37

THE COCKATIEL BEGINS a frantic pounding of its wings against the cage. Wild cries. I look up and out over the bay; against the grey sky, I see the languorous and perfect black V of Canada geese undulating south. Their soft honks come to us as if from far away. For a second it seems as if the top of the V wavers, begins to descend into the bay. The cockatiel's cries become more harsh and insistent. But the thin, open triangle snakes up and away and disappears beyond the point.

The cockatiel calms down. I take it out of the cage, and it sits on the table pecking reflectively at some Camembert on my lunch plate—shakes its head. God, says the cockatiel, I don't know what came over me. Lost my head for a second there. Those turkeys were talking wild rice and beansprouts in hot lagoons somewhere down south. Sounded fantastic!

Do you want to go? I ask. Just say the word.

Are you kidding? squawks the cockatiel. A thousand miles over enemy territory with every goddamn red-neck in the U.S.A. in a Cat hat firing twelve-gauge pellets out of his Ford pickup? Forget it. It's that kind of romanticism that destroys the call of the wild. Bullshit! The cockatiel spits out a dry edge of the Camembert contemptuously.

Why didn't they stop? I asked. It looked like the leader was ready to.

Ha! cried the cockatiel, they're all pussy-whipped like you. The males were talking about a quick feed of mussels and shrimp, but the women said they'd had a gut full of seafood, and if they didn't get someplace warm pretty soon the whole spring mating deal was cut off. Boy, did you see those ganders zoom up again quick smart! Primitive instincts. I must admit though, the id is not easily subdued. For a second I could just feel that sunlight on my wings and just taste the juice in those sprouts. When the hell is the sun going to appear in this country? I want to go home to Australia. I love a sunburnt country, a land of sweeping plains. The cockatiel puts one claw across its chest, patriotically. Of rugged mountain ranges, of droughts and flooding rains.

You're insane, I say, and walk away.

I think of packing up, giving the bird away. Taking the false passport and buggering off back to Australia. But I can't leave. Not without Yvonne. There's a great ragged hole in my life. I dipped out on her. Bloody insensitive bastard, I am. Didn't see what she needed. Took for myself, never gave.

The phone rings. I literally leap over a chair to grab it.

Hello?

I thought I'd drop by for a cup of tea, says Yvonne, very cool, not giving anything away. If that's convenient.

Yeah, I say, real cool, I'll be here.

I hang up. Jump straight up in the air, kick my heels, scream Whoopee! Grab the birdcage and dance about the room. I know I won't stuff up this time. It's a second chance. I'm going to be my perfect, considerate, thoughtful self. I'm going to toss off my shell forever.

It won't work, cries the cockatiel, bouncing about in its cage, I'm much more compatible with her than you are.

Bullshit, I sing to the bird, that's all the band could play, bullshit, they played it night and day.

38

I'M AS EXCITED AND NERVOUS as a kid on Christmas Eve. I've made little sandwiches, bought some chocolate cake. Got the kettle ready to boil, some Earl Grey already in the teapot. Five red roses in a vase.

She's late as usual. I'm scared she won't turn up. But she does. The VW van blats down the drive. I'm at the door waiting.

G'day, she says brightly, swinging past me and into the cabin. She can't get the nasal twang, but it's a good opening.

G'day, I say with exaggerated Aussie nasality. She walks to the kitchen table, takes in the display, looks back at me and grins.

You're crazy, O'Donnell, she says. And your letter. It was so pathetic it was sweet.

That was my tenth attempt, I say, I couldn't get it to sound right even then.

And you think you're a writer, Yvonne teases gently.

I'm not sure what I am, I reply.

Yvonne sits down. I get the kettle boiling. I'm on edge. I don't want to mess things up.

I missed you, I say, pouring the tea.

Yvonne picks up her cup. Her little finger points straight at me.

Why did you write yours truly at the end of the letter? Yvonne asks.

Isn't that the right way to do it? I reply.

You could have said, love, Jack, Yvonne suggests.

I wasn't sure you'd believe me, I say.

I don't think that's the problem, Yvonne says. It's more about intimacy. And you, you have to get out of this cabin more, get out and meet some people.

I'm silent for a second. I'm not too keen on the idea of getting out into the world. I'm scared they're waiting for me. But I know I have to if I'm ever going to be alive again.

What's the matter, Jack? Yvonne's voice is concerned.

I don't know whether I can get out into the world, I say. I know you're right. I don't know whether I'm ready for it or ready for you.

Yvonne gets up and comes around to me. She holds my face between her two hands.

I'm not going to mother you, Jack, she says, but I sure as hell love you, and I'm going to help you get over this as much as I can.

What if I can't, I say desperately, what if we end up fighting again?

It's a good bet we'll have our disagreements, Yvonne says, but if we've got this understanding, we'll be okay.

I grab her and hold her close. Jesus, I missed you, I say.

39

YOU DON'T GO OUT ENOUGH, Yvonne announces breathlessly, as soon as she is through the door. It's Friday. She's finished work for the week.

I have decided . . .

She takes off her duffle coat and puts both cool hands to my cheeks. Her eyes search mine after a brief kiss. Her lips are cool. Behind her, through the window, I see a few flakes of snow falling.

Decided what? I ask.

To ask some people around, she smiles.

Oh no! No way. I'm not interested.

Tonight! Yvonne's eyes gleam with delight at the surprise. I knew if I let you think about it you wouldn't want to. So. Spontaneous. Right now.

Tonight? No! I'm busy. I frantically search for excuses. The place is a mess. Look at it. Papers everywhere. Books. I haven't cleaned up here for ages.

Yvonne cups my face in her two cool hands. You've got to get out of yourself. You live like you're in a prison or something. I've asked some friends around.

I take her hands down from my face. Yvonne, I plead, I don't want a bunch of people coming around.

Too late! she cries gaily and steps into the living room. A second later the vacuum cleaner's high drone rises above talk. The bird shrieks and curses at the noise. But her jaw is set as she thrusts and retrieves the infernal machine over the carpet.

Yvonne's friends. Christ. A collection of encounter group ghoulies.

I'm leaving, I yell, leaning around the door.

What, says Yvonne over the hum of the vacuum cleaner. She turns it off.

I don't want visitors, I yell a bit too loudly. I'm going out.

Where? she cries. She's nonplussed. You can't. I've invited them.

Well you can just bloody well uninvite them, I state flatly.

I put on my coat.

You're being selfish, she yells, getting pretty riled up now.

Bullshit, I say, quaking inwardly a bit. I've never pushed this hard before. Usually I just go along with her, whatever she wants.

You're just trying to show how tough you are, she spits at me. Big male macho strong silent nonsense. Always gets his own way. She's warming up. So am I.

You didn't ask me beforehand, I argue. I don't like your friends.

Well that does it. She's romping and yelling now, pretty well fit to be tied. I hear I'm juvenile, paranoid, insensitive, selfish again, a few of the accusations get repeated in stuttering anger. The cockatiel flies to my shoulder, tweaks my ear. He's enjoying the barrage I'm getting. But while it makes my gut feel like jelly, I'm determined to stick it out. Stubborn as a mule, that's the Irish in me.

The cockatiel is no help.

Dear chap, offers the cockatiel, a bit of social company would be most enjoyable. You're a dull dog at the best of times. A party, a little social intercourse, good conversation, a little wine, perhaps some pâté, a good cheese. Don't be silly, old boy. She's quite right, you know. You can't live in this ridiculous existential isolation.

You shut your mouth, I yell at the cockatiel. Yvonne thinks I've yelled at her. There's a horrible pause.

What did you say? Yvonne screams, measuring each word slowly like a pound of cyanide.

I was talking to the bird, I say lamely.

The bird? Huh! I will not be insulted like that, Yvonne huffs and puffs herself into a great rage.

Ah, bugger the lot of you, I yell and walk out, slamming the door. And instantly regretting it.

I drive a couple of miles up to the local pub. Boy, they're depressing places. They want you to feel guilty about drinking and they're very successful. No open windows in case someone looks through and sees you sinning. You can't stand up at the bar. You've got to sit and stay like an obedient dog at your table, uniform little round tops covered in green to match the noxious beer. No singing, no cards, no joy, no fun. You can't walk around and socialize. You're supposed to sit and get joylessly sodden. No food except a few jars of pickled eggs in murky vinegar or dried-out ratshit pepperonis. Tonight it's early and dead quiet. Half a dozen Indian kids are messing about playing pool. They're pretty hammered. Joe Bob's not here. There's an old couple in the corner and the local bore and bludger, two in one, sitting closest to the bar. He tries to catch my eye, but I sit with my back to everybody. I feel terrible. Fighting with Yvonne. What an idiot I am. I don't know what came over me. Just felt run over and reacted like a dope. Wouldn't have hurt a bit to have those people around. Now I'm scared. That's it. Good-bye girl. I've lost her. It's over. I line up two beers. One of the Indian kids goes to the juke box and plays a tune. Sure enough it's the one. Gracie Slick. Jefferson Airplane. Blast from the past. Vietnam. RAR radio, Bien Hoa. Don't you want somebody to love, don't you need somebody to love. Total depression. I remember lying on my back and hearing it and feeling immensely sad. Yes Gracie, I do. Christ I'm damn near crying in my beer. Wouldn't you like somebody to love. Yes, I'm saying, damn near dying inside, yes. Ah Christ. You better find somebody to love. Ah Gracie. It's weird. Byzantine, I start to say to myself, Byzantine.

The door opens. I feel the cold rush at my back. I drain my beer.

Hi soldier, says a voice at my back. Buy me a drink?

Christ. It's Yvonne. I jump to my feet, knocking over the beer glasses.

I grab her and damn it, I'm crying like a kid, holding her and sobbing.

Christ I'm sorry, I say, Jesus I'm really sorry.

Hey, it's okay, she says gently. It was my fault. Let's go home, mate. Okay? Let's go home.

Of course it didn't happen like that at all.

I'll tell you straight before the cockatiel leaps in. I folded my cards pretty well straight away. Wimped right out. Sat up like a dog begging for a bone. Apologized. Helped her clean up. Made some fancy tucker in the kitchen, salmon sandwiches, crackers, oysters, cheese. Whipped out and bought pâtè, dip, wine and beer. Enjoyed every minute of it really. I think I'm changing.

A bunch of them turned up an hour later. Five women. Four guys. One sissy with a bow tie and glasses. Some visiting poet from Toronto. We blew some smoke. Yakkety yakked. There was the usual debate about Vietnam. Yvonne snuck it in, winking at me and enjoying our secret immensely. A pompous bigwig from the local college, who looked like Big Bird, was all for shooting communists, while a nasty little black-bearded union organizer who'd had a package tour to Moscow was all for the Viet Cong. Both of them looked as if they'd piss themselves if someone fired a shot. I kept quiet. Though it struck me how hypocritical Canadians were. God knows how they kept out of Vietnam. Instead, they tut-tutted over what a horror it was, sold a pisspot full of munitions to the Yanks, and accepted every freak and phony from the States who claimed to be a draft dodger. But I've learned to keep my mouth shut.

Two women called Gwen and Ellen arrived. They eyed me off suspiciously. Guilty of fucking up Yvonne in the first degree. Introduction. Gwen. Big boned, greying hair cut short, long dark blue dress, two hundred pounds, square, lively face, grey eyes, forty-five, maybe fifty, tough, and not convinced yet that I'm human. Ellen. Small, blondish, chirpy, bright blue eyes, big hoop earrings, about thirty-five, hard to tell, a grey dress suit with trousers. She's not as tough. Might think I'm okay.

I made myself busy rushing around with plates of snacks, poured wine, mixed drinks, kept out of the road. Except that at Yvonne's request, I pulled up my trousers and lowered my socks to show everybody the inherited convict leg-iron marks about my ankles. I swore it was true. So did Yvonne. Finally Gwen laughed, and then everybody got the joke and laughed their heads off. That took the pressure off.

We blared some Bob Dylan, some Rolling Stones out into the dope-laden air. Danced. They talked some more. I told them some jokes. They liked the Ned Kelly one. The dope got me going inside, deeper and deeper, slower and slower. I watched someone light a joint. It seemed to take endless hours as the flame grew and was moved closer and closer to the rolled cigarette. I winced when the coals glowed. Faces swam in and out of my vision like fishes in some huge fish tank.

There was Harris again in his pirouette of death, his *danse macabre,* smiling insanely as he turned, his body shocked and blasted by three bullets, his arms flailing as he turned, ever so slowly, grasping in the air for something, anything to grab hold of, anything to grip, to keep him upright, breathing and alive on this green earth. Suddenly he turned into a coin, spinning heads, tails, heads, tails; gargoyle faces appeared, bloody and insane, disappeared, appeared again. With a massive, internal, silent scream I fell through green and dark and endless jungle.

Actually, I was the life of the party. Fell asleep on the floor at ten o'clock. They just talked and danced, giggling around and about me, Yvonne says. She claims it was a great success. What the hell, I suppose that's what matters.

OBSERVE THE PERSPECTIVE and its blend with the colours of the clothes of the characters, cries the cockatiel. One ascetic claw trembling and outstretched, the bird balances itself precariously on the edge of my Breughel print of *The Peasant Dance*. Though the colours in this cheap print are far inferior to the original, it is nevertheless possible to perceive the animal vitality of these Flemish peasants, their arrogant sexuality balanced by the innocence of the ceremony. *Idiot savants*, of course, the lot of them. And here, the cockatiel taps with one claw at a man and a woman in the background, we have the classic dilemma. The perception of the sexes. Notice the woman is half in and half out of the doorway, while grasping both hands of the man.

So what? I ask.

Ahah, says the cockatiel. Is the woman pulling the man inside the house? Or is the man pulling the woman outside to dance?

Give me a look, I say, coming closer to the print.

I'd say the woman is pulling the man inside, I conclude.

Just so, chortles the cockatiel. Just so. My point precisely, a typical male perception. The female exerting her domestic power over the sense of community in the male, holding him back, enclosing him in her will. Yes.

But, the bird raises its claw high, if we were to ask a woman say, for example, that luscious piece of pulchritude who visits you, she would deny your perception. To her, this scene would show the man pulling the reluctant woman out of her necessary domestic duties into the circle to dance. Yes. I can assure you of that. The cockatiel nods quickly and turns back to the painting.

Sadly, the cockatiel adds, this is why we are obliged to live in constant emotional combat. Gender war. *Quelle condition fatale!* A tut, tut, tut, sound emerges slowly from the bird's beak as its head weaves slowly back and forth in a tragic gesture of despair.

When Yvonne comes in that night I take her to the painting, point out the two figures, ask her what's going on. She looks at me suspiciously.

Is this a trick question, O'Donnell? she demands.

No, I protest, I'm just interested in your view.

I hope, she says, that the man is pulling the woman out to dance, but I wouldn't, as you say, put the crown jewels on it. What do you think?

Yeah, I think you're right, I say, it's a tossup.

41

NOW THAT I'VE got to know her a bit, I've discovered Yvonne isn't perfect. It's a bit of a shock. Little things, like the thin and hardly perceptible row of hair on her upper lip. She uses wax to keep it out of sight. And the hairs in the bath after she's been shaving her legs are as gross as anything I produce. And she has this habit of giving a quick sniff and saying mmm when we're talking. And her crazy little nervous laugh. And she's always interminably late, on every occasion, every time. She'll come rushing in, her leather handbag swinging wildly, a plastic bag or two in her hand and say, breathlessly, I'm not late, am I? Once I said back to her, you're always bloody late. But that was because I'm starting to act like a house-husband, stuck at home all day. At least, that's what she tells me. She has so many women's committees and organizations she belongs to, she sometimes gets confused about which is which. It's even tougher to get it right, because the same women belong to all the organizations, and occasionally they'll forget who's the chairperson of which committee. At least she laughs about it. Most of the time she's in good humour, though when she's about to have her period she'll get pretty grouchy, and occasionally come out with a repulsive cold sore on her mouth. I pretend not to notice it, but it's a definite turnoff. I thought it was herpes at first, like in Vietnam, and that thought horrified her so much she went to the quack to make sure she was okay. And then came back and gave me a hell of a blast.

What we have in common, though, is the fact that we've both

been washed up here, come to rest together on this island, debris from the world swung in on the tide. We recognize that in each other. I don't mind that she doesn't like fishing, or going to the pub to drink beer, or playing cards. And she just won't watch hockey on TV. I love the Broad Street Bullies of Philadelphia, bashing heads and sliding about together so much on skates that no one can get planted to land a solid punch. It's a joke. But Yvonne goes off to the loft to read when I turn the TV on. She seems quite happy about it, too. Maybe it's part of our separate but joined lives.

But I'm damned if I'll ever get her to say "G'day mate" properly. She just doesn't have a proper "a" vowel. She'll say G'di meet or G'di mite, and even try to put a nasal twang in it, but it always sounds wrong.

I don't say much about all this to her. I don't want to hurt her. But it really pisses me off sometimes when she wears these long earrings and eye shadow and opens her blouse down to her navel so you can just about see all her tits. She says she likes to jangle. I say she looks like a bloody tart. All she does is get a laugh out of my worried glances. She shakes her head at my pathetic male attitudes most times. Though the other night when I asked for a second cup of tea she gave me a real jolt. I made the tea, turned on the hockey and watched Dave the Hammer bloodying up some Montreal Canadien. Whoopee, I yelled, get him Dave. I called out to ask for a cup of tea, which Yvonne brought without any trouble. But when I yelled out to ask her for a second cup, there was no answer. I walked out into the kitchen, and there she was banging the dishes together in the sink with incredible passion.

Any more tea? I asked quietly.

Yvonne turned and heaved a bowl full of dishwater on my chest.

Get it yourself, she yelled and burst out crying.

What's the matter? I went to hold her in my arms.

Don't you touch me, she screamed, just because I love you doesn't mean you own me. Get your own tea. I'm going home.

And with that outburst, she grabbed her bag and ran out the door, slamming it with great force behind her.

All that over a cup of tea? I asked no one in particular.

You male idiot, cried the bird.

Ahah, I cried, I know more than you this time! She's done her nut over those idiots beating each other on the hockey game. I felt very wise and insightful.

I waited a while and phoned her.

Yes, she said, tensely.

It's the hockey, right? I cried triumphantly, the sounds of the fight and the crowd? That's the trigger. I get it. It won't happen again. I won't watch hockey any more.

No, you idiot, O'Donnell, she laughed.

What? I said, What the hell upset you then?

It is your master of the house trip, stupid, cried Yvonne.

One cup of tea too many. Get your own damn tea.

Oh, I said, I guess I won't ever get this right.

Well, Yvonne replied. It's not just you. As long as we're both trying it's okay.

It was not much consolation to me. But I knew I had to let her come to me. I hung up the phone.

Two hours later I heard the VW blatting down the road. I felt strangely calm.

Things are working out okay.

42

WHERE DID THE COCKATIEL get that blush on his cheek, that pink roseate flush, that unknown stigmata? With this bird, perched now at dawn on the brass rails of my double bed, its black beady eyes observing Yvonne sleeping innocently beside me, the covers down, so that with each slow soft breath her exposed breasts tremble ever so slightly, I have my suspicions. Surely this cockatiel was perched high in the Tree of Knowledge in the Garden of Eden when the snake arrived with its cozening ways. Surely the cockatiel leaned down to innocent Eve and whispered its dry rattle of encouragement as, uncertain, she held the apple in her hand. Surely this cockatiel, too, bit into that forbidden fruit at the same time as Eve made her fatal mistake. And it knew, then, instantly, the sin of sexual awareness, of the naked and seductive curves and hollows of human flesh.

And for its sins, now carries, in perpetual pink shame, the stigmata, the blush of embarrassment on its feathered cheek.

Pervert! Voyeur! I call softly to the bird as its black eyes fix unwaveringly on the pink circles of Yvonne's breasts.

You! snarls the cockatiel with gaping and aggressive beak thrust at me, have the mind of Oliver Cromwell!

43

I LIE ON MY BACK looking up at the red cedar ceiling. Its whorls and knots are ever changing. This morning there are all heads. Some whole, some shot to pieces. Some distorted. I must conceive them myself, create everything every time. Like Adam, I name what I see. The knots, the grain, never giving a full head, but a curve here, a few lines there, suggesting the shape. Three Grecian whorls with curls and blind eyes. Three Fates. Yvonne is dressing for work. She makes of it a very normal event. I cannot think about getting up. I do not want to move. If I look again I can see gargoyles, horrible faces now, twisted mouths, misshapen eyes, the leers of the dead, the faces of Cong, dead and piled monstrously for the body count, Quasimodo pain and surprise and madness frozen into this red cedar ceiling. She asks me if I want breakfast. The alarm clock is set for 7:30. No. I hate it. Interruptions in the true state. The bell that summons thee to wasp waste every morning. I look for familiar faces in the red cedar. Wacker with a too large mouth, laughing. My father with a bitter grin. I would like to record all these. I would like to paint these faces every day. I have to. You must sometimes force symmetry upon the world, it's so fucking lazy.

44

THIS EVENT I'm about to recall is so grotesque I'm not sure I didn't dream it. The cockatiel, of course, figures again in its most perverted character. A real Jekyll and Hyde this feathered freak.

Yvonne and I had just made love in front of the Orley stove. Cozy, warm, the red flame in the window encouraged the performance. We're lying there on our backs, naked and half-asleep, afterwards, in that drained and pleasant postsensual drowse everybody knows, when the cockatiel begins to rattle its cage. I look up, and there's this feathered frenzy, the bird doing multiple loops about its perch, flashing its wings, raising and lowering its crest. It emerges from the cage, does some fast zooms and dives, centred on Yvonne, and then hovers and lands on her shoulder. It whispers in her ear and bats its wings very softly about her face. Half-asleep, she smiles and stretches languidly. This sets the bird to furious muttering. I hear snippets. Your skin is soft as fresh seed, your ears more lovely than . . . your breasts as perfect as persimmons. And so on. I'm not registering properly, until I see the bird begin to stroke Yvonne's nipples with soft beats of its feathered wings. As they rise, the bird chirps and begins to nibble lightly at each peach pink protuberance. Yvonne stirs again. I realize suddenly, the bird is trying to make love to her. I reach out and grab the little sick freak in my right fist. It struggles and bites at my thumb.

You little pervert, I cry, you sick little shit.

Let me go, you big ox, hisses the bird, struggling to get a bite hold on my thumb. I get up and shove the bird back in its cage, a bit roughly, and it tumbles in spread wing confusion to the bottom of the cage. But it raises its head and screams at me.

You sadist! Performing right in front of me. Do you think I enjoy this enforced celibacy? Do you think I like this monastic self-flagellation, this denial of the flesh, this vicious truncation of my natural desires? You inhuman, insensitive brute! Throwing your carnal and libertine behaviour right in my face. What sick mind came up with this sensual torture?

The bird moans and tucks its head under its wing and rocks sadly back and forth on the gravel paper at the bottom of its cage.

I'm a bit stunned. The thought of the bird wanting sex throws me somewhat. I suppose it's only natural. But what am I supposed to do? Let it get at Yvonne? I lock the cage door.

I get a blanket and cover Yvonne. She sighs a little and reaches for me. Ah, maybe later love, I say, with a guilty glance at the cage where the bird rocks back and forth, emitting the occasional heartrending sob.

45

WHAT WAS YOUR CAMP LIKE? Yvonne asks me one night. We're just sitting there by the fire like an old married couple.

In Vietnam? I ask.

Yes.

I haven't told her much. It's all getting written, in my notebooks shoved in a drawer. Every day a couple of pages, usually criticized instantly by my resident literateur, the bloody cockatiel. He thinks it's abysmal, but as Ezra Pound, that well known fascist crazy says, don't trust any joker's opinion who hasn't written a pretty good book himself. So stuff the critics, and particularly, stuff the cockatiel. I'm sick of its superior academic arrogance.

Basically life was pretty boring, I tell Yvonne. I'm surprised it's that easy to begin to talk about it. I'd been afraid to tell her too much. A lot of it is just sick and crazy to anyone who wasn't there.

How, she says.

So I launch into a description. We lived under tents. Six men on campbeds. Day after boring day. Behind a perimeter of barbed wire and sandbags. It either rained so heavily, so suddenly, that everything was instantly soaked, or it was dry and dusty. Mainly, though, it rained. I now know what they mean by buckets full. We got totally drenched. Everything was moist. The ground turned into thick red mud. Our feet had constant tinea or worse. Growths between your toes, under your arms, in your crotch. A kind of rot. Everything was rotting. You ate food quick smart; it was usually horrible tinned muck. Even when they cooked it, it all went to a blank mush. A variety of horrible insects thrived in the moisture: spiders, scorpions, no names. We used to catch them to have fights between them in buckets. Have bets on them. Kids' stuff. A lot of kids' stuff. We used to chant War is a bore, war is a whore, war is a snore, any kind of dumb rhyme. Someone'd be lying there and start it out, and it'd go on until one bloke came out with a stupid rhyme, one that didn't fit like war is a door, and then we'd all throw boots at him. We spent all our money on beer, got drunk a lot, sang, bullshitted about home and girls. Told a lot of lies. We played cards but we got sick of it. Gambling, like pontoon, or poker for pennies, soon got pretty dull. We gave it a miss. I remember a few of the blokes down the row of tents got into a stoush, a bit of a punch up, they were so pissed off and bored. Nothing too serious, but the CO cut off everybody's beer ration. Now that was serious. Harris, our tent pisstank, was most indignant. If they're gonna treat us like dogs, let's act like dogs. You blokes in on it? he cried. It was a challenge. So we did. We barked and yelled at each other instead of talking. Yelp for salt in the mess tent. Growl for sugar. It was kind of funny, though the officers got pissed off. At night the whole camp started to howl like dogs. Hurroow. Hurroow. The officers raced about from tent to tent with flashlights, threatening us, but as soon as they left off we'd howl again. Hurroow. Hurroow. They paraded us all and threatened us with all sorts of stuff, no leave, court-martial, the lot. But we howled at night for three nights until they gave up finally, gave us back our beer, and the dogs left the camp.

Yvonne is shaking her head and laughing. I start to smile myself. There were some good times. I tell her about the cricket match. Just the mention of the game has her laughing. Canadians don't have a clue about how intricate the game is. It's a joke to them. Like baseball to Aussies. Anyhow, there was this lieutenant who fancied himself as a batsman, bit of a Don Bradman, he reckoned. He wasn't too too bad, really. But he got up our noses with his left elbow well up, straight down the flight of the ball. Even had his white cricket boots on and a white shirt. Bit too much for the blokes. So it was the monthly inter-squad game, and this looey's in there making a few cautious runs. Everybody else was gloriously slogging. Cross-batting and belting the ball and getting clean bowled, and he's there, tap, tapping, all polish and formality. Wacker got an idea, sent Harris off to find a dummy grenade from the training tent. Harris sneaked it to Wacker who sneaked it to the bloke at fine leg, who walked in with it at the change of over, handed it to the bowler—Keg Tindall, I think it was. So he ran and heaved this down the pitch, and we yelled, Grenade! and hit the dirt, and all the other bastards—fielders, umpires, batsmen, wicketkeeper—hit the ground. And the dummy grenade did a low bounce and took out the lieutenant's middle stump. Clean bowled the bastard. There was a bit of strife over that. They tried to pin it on Harris, but they couldn't. The lieutenant was very pissed off. But then we got a call and half the blokes had to hustle out on patrol, and that was the end of that.

What about patrols? Yvonne asks.

I'll tell you another time, I say, let's watch the news.

46

BEETHOVEN DAMN NEAR MAKES ME CRY. How did a no-hoper like me get introduced to that mighty artist? Yvonne, of course. I've been doing a kind of a fast course in growing up with her. It started with an argument. She came out with this statement that boys make war and men make art. Of course I bristled at that. Even though it's true we were boys over there. Poor no-hopers picked up off the streets or found diddling against the wind in dumb shit jobs like cane cutting, grape picking, station jackaroos. We were the nigger boys of Australia. The poor bastards without connections. But the fighting we had to do, I told Yvonne straight out, took a lot of guts. She just looked at me. She doesn't understand. Bits of it she gets, but not the whole bloody picture. Why should she? She's got her own chamber of horrors. She can no more imagine me in Vietnam that I can imagine some man belting her across the face time after time.

Anyhow, she brought over this tape player and a couple of speakers and blasted Beethoven at me. I can't remember which piece it was, probably the *Fifth*. That's my favourite still. I was bored to begin with. Couldn't get into it at all. But I played it again and again until the cassette started to give out that slurring gasp and I had to buy another tape. Beethoven's got it all. Somehow the balance between the quiet little lyrical bits, like a few drops of water, falling reflectively, and the great bursts of affirmation, like, yes, living and dying mate, that's the story. It's both sides of the coin, the pain and the pleasure, the beauty and the horror all mixed into one. It's Vietnam, the jungle birds, beautiful with their songs in the quiet dawn and the occasional flash of colour in the rich green foliage, and then the hideous blast of a mortar or the nightmare boom of a land mine and some poor bastard's legs all torn white and red, and the constant screaming. And the grotesque laughter at some other stupid moment, black as hell, but somehow funny. It's as if he knew it, knows it all, that this business of being alive is a two-sided jubilation, terror and joy separated by a thin membrane for no good reason and swinging in the wind like a flag, one side blowing then the other. And somehow Beethoven's above it all, orchestrating, directing the whole symphony so the quick sharp bits balance with the solemn deep rolls, and it all fits together as if it's natural, no sweat, easy as pie, look, no hands, Mum, and you just wonder at the mind that could put it all together, could conceive of it, put it down in all its complexity, and have it last all this time until now, on this island, for a bloke who never heard it before and who suddenly says, yes, that's it, that's the best, that's the pattern I recognize now you've shown me, that's how it works, that's the truth, bugger me, you've got the whole story there, Ludwig.

And, of course, there's Yvonne sitting over there, with that smile on her face, doing her Pygmalion trip on me yet again. Enjoying what she's creating. But I'm grateful, not resentful, and when I found out Beethoven, the poor old bastard, was deaf, you could've done the old feather trick. I mean I've got every faculty pretty well tuned in at high speed and what the fuck have I made? War, not art. It'd bring tears to a glass eye.

47

WHAT WERE PATROLS LIKE? she asks again, leaning on one elbow, her eyes moving slowly over my face, as if she's memorizing it, recording each detail.

I don't want to talk about Vietnam. It's become a series of images fading in importance. I don't reply.

You can tell me, she says softly, I won't be shocked.

Oh yeah, I think, not a touch of shock in seeing bodies blown up, grey intestines in the red mud, a man with his leg blown off, screaming, flopping about like a landed fish. No. This is not the time.

If you talk about it, she adds, it won't be as terrible. You won't have those nightmares. Trust me. She comes close and holds me.

Okay, I think angrily. You want to know, lady, you want an idea of madness, of horror.

Most of the time nothing much happened, I begin. A day or two before the patrol we stopped taking showers or washing up. Stops the smell. And we ate Vietnamese food. Rice and fish. Same reason. We usually went out at night, but often I'd be so scared I'd have diarrhea or puke. This was real cowboys and Indians. They gave us Preniliquin, a kind of quinine, for malaria. As in a mass, Double Barrel literally put it on our tongues once a week. The mosquitoes were really bad. We also had this mosquito repellent in a green bottle. Probably World War II stuff from New Guinea. It was so bad it raised welts on your face and hands and your lips swelled up. We took a couple of ration packs. We ate the peanut butter in the rations first off to gum up our guts. Nothing'd move in your bowels for days. It was like swallowing concrete. At the end of the patrol we'd drink the grape juice. It sent you running to the latrines. We didn't get resupplied by helicopter like the Yanks did. Usually ten or twelve of us, stumbling and slipping along some dark muddy trail for two or three days. Thick jungle undergrowth on either side. A line of blind men. We had our FN clips of twenty, two taped together, one upside-down, for quick exchange. The AK 47 the VC had was a better weapon, though. The first round had nylon spikes on the bullet to clean out the barrel. They'd thought through what the jungle was like, how to fight in it and survive. We'd had some pretty savage training at Canungra. Mean bastards. NCO's thumping and yelling as we went through their mock VC villages. Most of us got technically killed there. The sergeant got a kick out of screaming at us as we made some fatal mistake with a booby trap or a punge hole or some other horrible bloody thing. We learnt pretty quick, though. Some of the poor bloody Yanks only got two or three days' training and then flew straight into a firefight.

Yvonne puts her head down on the pillow beside me. I wonder if she's understanding all this. But now I've got an urge to talk, to go over the bits and pieces, the fragments of images welling up in my brain. I tell her about the rumour that the tigers followed the sound of firefights for a free meal, how you never walked through a gate or a hole in a fence or any obvious opening; how we shot the rats in the rice paddies and ate them; how we called them rice bunnies. About the heavy rain soaking through your wrapped-up poncho. Of being scared, terrified, so you could hardly move at night set up in ambush, waiting for the counterambush the VC invariably had in wait because somehow they knew every move we made or planned to make. About the beautiful butterflies six inches across and all the colours of the rainbow. And the magnificent flash of colour of jungle birds. About the leeches in your armpits and crotch and the four-foot vine snakes—thin as a bootlace and poisonous—hanging from the branches. Heaven and hell. The days of slogging through mud and the utter horror of a thirty-second firefight, everybody blazing away in mindless terror, freaking out, sometimes shooting our own men by mistake. Of the Willy Peter, white phosphorous grenade, the size of a small can of peas and the vc burning and screaming from its explosion. Of our own homemade napalm, petrol and Ivory snowflakes in a can with a fuse and detonator. Of the strange silence after a contact, the throb of your blood in your ears loud as a drum and someone hit, his blood merging indistinguishably with the orange-red mud. About coming upon a vc cache, five sacks of U.S. Red Cross rice and, incredibly, two sacks of Aussie mail, some opened, and finding in the rest, a birthday card for Harris from his grandmother. Weird. Byzantine.

Yvonne utters a small sigh. I turn to look at her. She gives a little snore. She's fast asleep. I shake my head. It's probably better this way.

48

THE COCKATIEL READS as voraciously as it eats. It perches on the lower ledge of a lectern, in the bay window, turning the pages with a querulous left claw. How does this bird know how to read? A giant genetic hiccup in its parents? A mixup with transmigration? A massive mitosis explosion in its cell development? A mutation from the 1950s British atomic tests at Maralinga? That fucked up a lot of central Australia. I do not know. I suspect the presence of multifold personalities from several ages; its hatreds and prejudices are so clear, its knowledge and taste so developed, albeit eccentrically, that it functions as a decadent fifty-year-old literate bohemian.

Now here! says the cockatiel, turning to me, its crest raised in anger. Here, it taps a paragraph, is something that should never have been printed. A dog? Speaking? My God! And thinking! Listen to this. It's barbarous. And this other book. A cat with perception? About God?

Good God, a savage'd have better taste than that. This is unbelievable!

You're so negative, I say. I'm going to bed.

Okay, says the cockatiel, absorbed in the next page, leave the cage door open.

49

YOU ADMIRED WACKER, Yvonne says. She leans forward on the table, her face cupped in both hands. Her wineglass is empty. I am not sure it's a question. It's more an invitation. I fill her glass. And mine. It's some South Aussie red. A Cabernet Sauvignon. Rich and fruity. It's show and tell time. Tell me something about yourself so I can see who you are. I'm not biting. I don't answer. I begin to clean up the dishes. I never thought it'd come to this. Here I am, the bloody cook. Baked salmon, scalloped potatoes, beans amandine, beetroot. Yvonne brings the wine. She can't cook worth a damn and I'd rather not eat her food. Christ, she eats rabbit stuff, all salads and greens. A man's appendix'd end up tripling in size. So we've come to this arrangement. It's a strange one, but that's my life. Male pride down the drain. Arse about teakettle. Instead of me turning up to her place with flowers and wine to get fed, she turns up at my place with wine. She's too smart to bring me flowers yet, but, Christ on a crutch, that could happen. If me old mates could see me doing things this way, they'd piss themselves laughing. At least I don't wear a bloody apron. Yet. Though I do get a fair earful of "how's your day been" bullshit from her side. All these women getting banged up by men. Hiding out with their nippers in the Crisis House. I listen now. I've got an interest in it. Couple of times I've felt like finding out where the bastards live and giving those blokes a good belting to straighten them up. But that's pointless too.

Did you? says Yvonne, hanging in there like grim death.

What, I say.

Admire Wacker, she says impatiently.

Why?

Jesus, I should've known. Here we go, down in my boots again scrounging around for an answer.

I don't know, really, half the answers to the questions she asks. They're all directed below the belt, into some fine-tuned emotional radio I'm just starting to build.

He was tough, I say, but generous. And no, that's not enough.

We was mates, I add, and I know to a girl, let alone a Canadian, that doesn't make sense. They're not into mateship. Male bonding, Yvonne calls it, and that pisses me off, as if it's that simple or that clear.

I could rely on him, I say, he'd be there.

Emotionally, Yvonne asks, and suddenly I'm getting angry.

Look, I say, you'd never understand. We weren't bloody poofters. We were very close friends—mates. It's an Australian thing. In the war you look after each other. He'd bail me out of the clink, give me his last dollar, stand back to back with me in a fight, listen to me gripes, cheer me up, keep me straight, crack a joke. All of that.

That's love, Yvonne says quietly, you loved him. Admit it, O'Donnell.

Christ, I say, angry and exasperated. Yeah. If you want to put it that way. Yeah. I loved him. Bugger it. Okay? I loved him.

I glare at her, but she puts that grin on her face, and I realize I've got a bloody tea towel in one hand. Jesus, it's hard being macho with her. I toss it on the table, sit down, pour another glass of red wine. She gets up, walks around the table, picks up my wineglass, sips, leans to kiss me and spurts a little wine into my mouth. It's exciting, intimate, trusting. She kisses me, open mouthed, her tongue softly exploring mine. She stands back.

I love you, she says with that smile. I want to be your mate.

Is that possible? Mates are men, I tell her.

She just laughs.

She still can't pronounce mate correctly. But I'll ignore that. I think she loves me.

That's a bit sexually weird. It's not the same thing, I say jokingly.

She puts her arms around me, whispers in my ear. Shall I save you from your homosexual tendencies?

You bet, I say, feeling a rush. Fuck the dishes. We run up into the loft.

50

WHAT'S THE MATTER WITH YOU? the cockatiel demands.

The page lies blank and forbidding on my desk.

Problems, I reply. Blood. Guilt. Yvonne. Writing. Questions. Pushing the craft beyond my skills. Money. Death. Human Nature. The Government. The Cosmos.

Life is strife, pontificates the cockatiel. We are constantly in a process of *Heilgeschichte.*

What? I say.

Salvation history! states the bird.

Axis agea. The three ages of Father, Son, and Spirit. Though our Karma is independent of these factors, of course.

What are you talking about?

The bird lifts its head.

We go up. We go down on the merry-go-round. Life is a bitch and then we die. Ixion's wheel. According to our Karma and what we do with it. Time is merely the flow in which we exercise our potential.

I check the Courvoisier. No. The bird is not drunk. It's true then. This bird has had earlier lives. Or thinks it has. Who has it been? Or are they not specific? I've read about the Buddhist notion of purging the fleshly desires so that one attains Nirvana. Is this bird moving through one personality at a time on some journey of the soul? Right before my eyes?

As a matter of fact, the cockatiel begins, I'm starting to wonder if you've even taken the first step.

51

I GET UP EARLY, leave Yvonne curled up under the down cover. It's cold. Outside the ground is frozen. The temperature dropped last night like a stone, the heat sucked out by a clear sky. Without the usual soft grey clouds to blanket the earth, there's no protection.

I start the woodstove with cedar kindling. In this weather you have to roar it alive or it blows back down the frozen chimney. Soon it's an orange wave dancing behind the glass door.

The cockatiel sleeps in a ball of fluffed feathers. I don't wake it because it'll bitch about the cold.

I pull on my boots, throw my red Mackinaw on and walk out, the frozen ground crunching slightly, like sugar granules, underfoot. The sea is dark oily grey, waiting, ominous.

I have some decisions to make. I can't keep living like life's a crazy floating two-up game. I can't keep grabbing and moving on. I have to find something to hang onto, some kind of peg or marker or buoy to measure the angles and approaches.

I walk down the shore trying to make up my mind. Marry Yvonne. Find some kind of job. It's all frightening, the thought of permanence, commitment. I'm not capable of it. I'm too restless, too much wildness in my blood. But if I don't, what then?

I climb up some rocks and come upon a little shallow lake, a slough they call it over here. Something moving on the middle catches my eye. I push through the bare alder winter branches towards the edge. The surface shimmers, frozen an inch or so overnight. As I get clear of the alders I see it. A large bird. A Canada goose, I think, in the middle of the slough, lying flat, as if very tired, its brown wings spread wide and low. It slowly flips and collapses. There's a little flash of white cheek on the dark head. Below the dark brown wings a light-coloured chest heaves and settles. It flaps vainly again and collapses. It's caught, trapped somehow in the ice. Strange. Could it have been sleeping on the water, and the ice formed quickly, trapping its wide webbed feet? Surely it can break loose. But no. It flaps slowly once more and lies there. What the hell is it doing here when every other sane and reasonable Canada goose, brant and duck has flown south? It's quite weird. I think of turning back to the cabin. I'm not going to risk going out on the ice to get it. Nature has its way of dealing with mistakes. You pay your money and take your chances. Yvonne, I know, would be crying and racing around in panic already at the goose's dilemma. I don't. Maybe I'm still a cold bastard. What the hell, there's nothing I can do. I'd go straight through the ice and down into who knows what depth of water.

I start to turn back, but the damn bird gives this pathetic flap and utters this soft, lost cry. Now I'm stuck. I can't go back and leave it. I'm hooked into its fate, damn it. Everything catches you, traps you into its connection. You just can't get free.

I crash my way through the alders to the nearest point on land to the goose. It panics a bit at the noise, but it's so tired, so worn out with its struggle to get free, that it collapses once more into a light brown heap, its wings spread wide.

I put one foot on the ice, slowly increasing the weight. The ice is dark and opaque. Three cracks instantly star and run out from my boot. Damn. I've got to go out prone.

I lie down, spread my arms and legs on the ice to distribute the weight. It seems okay. I inch my way out over the frozen slough towards the goose, little by little.

I'm scared it's going to suddenly shatter, dump me in the frozen water, leave me panicking to get to shore, grabbing at nothing solid. Damn it, I could drown right next to the bloody goose. My goose cooked, or rather frozen. It seems so ridiculous, I start to giggle nervously. The bird now sees me and flaps a few frantic times. Of course it doesn't know my intentions are liberal, philanthropic, humane. I get closer. The bird twists its head, its dark eyes beady and fearful. The white cheeks flash an instant.

Closer still, I reach out with my right hand under the light grey belly feathers. The bird twists and tries to peck. My hand closes on the scaly legs. They're caught all right. I can't release them by pulling. I'll have to smash the ice somehow. I reach back to my pocket for a pocketknife, open it, inch closer. The goose flaps its wings, the pinions batter at my arms and face. I grab the legs with my left hand and stab, stab with the knife at the ice about the bird's feet. Harder and harder, I beat with the knife. And crack. Suddenly the ice caves in underneath me. Splash. I'm floundering, shocked cold out of breath, the goose legs in one hand, the knife dropped. My feet kick with the boots and, wonderful, they hit soft mud. Bubbles of stench rise about me. I stand up, spluttering and frozen, waist deep in the slough, the ice broken in long stars all away from me. I kick and wade through the fragmented ice, cradling the soft goose, now struggling weakly against my chest. It only weighs a couple of pounds. I feel its heart beat. I'm shivering, half from the cold, half from the shock, when I wade onto the shore.

I sit and stroke the marvellous dark down neck of this bird. After a minute or so it comes to life. I hold it up, release its legs, and with two powerful beats of the grey-brown pinions it takes off, rises higher and higher above the slough, goes beyond, out over the sea, half-gliding, free. I feel good. I have a story to tell Yvonne that'll bring that approving and lovely wide smile to her face. I hope she believes me.

52

THE HERRING FLEET is rioting out there in the bay. Maybe fifty boats manoeuvring day and night for position, waiting for the signal to rush the skiffs into place, drop the nets, pull the ripe herring in by the ton. Squeeze out the roe. They come from all over. Meanwhile they're drinking and yelling and cursing; day and night, jockeying about. In the morning the tide line is a mess of tangles, styrofoam, beer and rum bottles, cans, condoms, a ton of garbage. They make a pisspot, these guys, in just a few hours. They sell the roe to Japan at some astronomical figure. Some delicacy, an aphrodisiac, maybe. The deck hands come ashore at all hours, foraging, waiting for the call on the VHF to let it all rip. They run out of supplies, but don't dare leave to fill up in case the opening is called.

Barbarians! declares the cockatiel, bartering the eggs of the young for money. I can see how the human race has sunk to its present level of disgrace. Eggs, traditionally, have been in any significant culture, sacred. Noisy louts. And the mess. Oh, it's just too much for anyone of a sensitive nature.

I point out that he likes caviar, eats it; that caviar is sturgeon roe. Eggs. Ha. I've got him.

Preposterous argument, cries the cockatiel, they're too small and unformed at that stage to be anything but food. God, your face is a mess this morning. Why don't you shave and clean up. You look positively revolting. Like a Russian peasant.

The cockatiel flies in a huff into its cage.

Two fishermen banged on my door last night about six.

Wanted to buy some food, any booze I had. I told 'em I didn't have any spare. The big one pushed the door open and walked in. Pulled out a roll of fifties, peeled off two, offered them to me. His face was familiar. Round, pink, white eyebrows. Had a black tuque. Couldn't place him. The other one followed him in. Dark face. I didn't like their attitude. Used to getting their way. I moved over to where the twelve-gauge stood by the stove. They understood that, but didn't move. I gave them a few cans, a dozen eggs, bread, a bit of other stuff. Threw in a bottle of Scotch and six beer.

Do I know you? Baby Face asked. Slight American accent.

I hope not, I said. Here, take this stuff and piss off.

Not friendly, said the dark one. Brooklyn twang.

I like my privacy, I said slowly and clearly. Don't come back.

Baby Face gave a tiny grin. With a shock I recognized him. Jesus. He was the bloke in Vietnam. The civilian who questioned me. Probably CIA. I reached out and took up the shotgun. I was scared.

What's the problem? asked Baby Face.

You, I said. You're in my house and I want you out.

Baby Face didn't move. He was not scared. He'd been there. He knew how hard it was for normal people to shoot someone.

I know you from somewhere, said Baby Face, San Diego? Hawaii? Vietnam?

Get the fuck out, I said, levelling the shotgun at his groin.

C'mon, said the dark one. He was scared. He grabbed the food and booze. He didn't want any trouble. Baby Face was the tough one.

Okay. Take it easy, said Baby Face, slowly walking backward to the door. I followed them outside. The dark one ran. I put one shot, Bam, high over their heads. Both hit the ground. Yeah, they'd been in Vietnam. They both got up and ran off to the beach. I stayed up all night just in case Baby Face came back. He looked like the type. The cockatiel woke up and I told it what had happened.

Christ Almighty, said the cockatiel, the only exciting incident in this boring life we lead and you let me sleep through it. I'd have had no trouble taking the big one, but I doubt you'd have been able to handle the dark one. Just as well you chickened out.

They called the opening at midnight. It was bedlam. Motors,

VHFs, curses, loudspeakers, shouts, lights flying here and there. I went out and watched hundreds of dark silhouettes clustering in the bay as they hauled tons of ripe silver flashes into their skiffs.

By seven in the morning the whole bay was deserted. A line of garbage a foot thick wound for a mile or more along the high tide line. The sea gulls were madly gobbling at dead herring and thick dark roe and other detritus. The stink of death and decay was everywhere. I knew that they'd found me. The penny had finally dropped, the red light on the computer flashed. Baby Face would eventually remember something. The flash card would turn up my face. He'd put something together. The only thing I could do was run. But to where? And leave Yvonne? No. Baby Face might never twig. Probably forgotten already in a haze of money and booze. What did he know, anyhow? No. There was no point in taking off. And there was Yvonne. I wouldn't leave her. Not now. But still that nagging sense of being at risk. Damn it. If it wasn't for Yvonne I'd be off and hidden in a day. She's making me stand out. I resent it and need it, all at the same time.

53

Yvonne has taken over my life. Not to mention the damned bird. Eased in, sneaked by my guard. I now have both of them on my mind. If Yvonne doesn't phone I start to worry. Has she had an accident? Got herself in some psychological trouble? Met some other man? Finally worked out how she'd be better off without me? Stuff like that. It gets you down. If the cockatiel doesn't bitch about something, I'm concerned about his health. More, they're dragging me out, putting me out there in the open. Like Yvonne, dramatically organizing lunch, in town, where I go to different supermarkets every two weeks for supplies. I'm super cautious. Hardly ever repeat a pattern. Particularly now that Baby Face has surfaced. I shop at different stores each time. Keep out of the busy times when the stores are full. It's cautious, sensible. But luncheon. Pretentious shit. Luncheon with Yvonne, and, it turns out, two of her Crisis Centre friends. She wants to show me off to them again, I suppose. Explain what she's been doing these last months. I'm not keen on the idea. I'm afraid I'll blurt out some male statement and get creamed. I'm very careful usually, but the horror's always there under the surface. Worse, I'll run into someone or something that'll blow my cover. But I go, anyhow.

I dither about a bit in Nanaimo, walk up and down the main streets. They used to be cobblestoned. You can see the little bits under the black top. But it's a place of no identity. Old coal town. No signs of that left. A mess of blank-faced architecture, rambling streets. Bathtub Capital of the World, a sign says.

Once a year a bunch of maniacs sitting in outboard-powered bathtubs cross thirty miles of the strait to Vancouver. True. The mayor dresses like a pirate, and I can't decide whether he's a stupid fool or an intellectual fool, taking the mickey out of this nothing little place he's supposed to be promoting. It has a wonderful setting, safe harbour, islands, parks, but they've buggered it all up. The red-necks run everything, and there is no man-made thing of beauty anywhere.

I turn into the pub we're meeting at; Yvonne's van is parked outside. I've lost count of the Save The Fill-in-the-Blank stickers she has plastered all over it. A myriad of clichés. I suggested she get a Save Everything sign, but she got a bit hostile and hurt. There they are, three of them in a corner. Ellen and Gwen. I relax a bit. Yvonne rushes up to me, a hug, a whisper, I was afraid you weren't going to make it. For you, I whisper, I'll dine with the witches of hell.

We talk, or more, I listen, answer a question or two. Their grant application is in. They work or die on its success, all three of them. Movies. I haven't seen *Five Easy Pieces.* Haven't seen any movies except the occasional one on the TV Yvonne insisted I borrow from her. They love *Five Easy Pieces.* Think it's a breakthrough. Jack Nicholson learned a lesson, they say. Our hamburgers and fries arrive. More beer. They laugh at my impressions of Nanaimo. Agree. More. Tell me it's worse. Rundown. Unemployed. Drugs. A nasty undercurrent to the whole place. Suddenly, a voice. Want to buy you girls a drink. We turn and there's Baby Face, the deck hand, a bit drunk, spending his herring money. What the hell is he doing here? Has he worked out where he's seen me?

What would you girls like? he says with a bit of a slur. He throws a red fifty onto the table. There's a weird silence. I look at the picture on the back of the fifty. A circle of Mounties on horses, facing inwards, their lances at the ready. A Newfie firing squad, someone told me once. I feel like I'm standing in the middle. I think of getting up, telling him to piss off, brazening it out, ignoring the fact I recognize him.

Whatever you like, girls, Baby Face says expansively.

Nothing, thank you, says Gwen very tightly. Baby Face grins.

C'mon, says Baby Face, you girls like a drink. You don't have to sit with queers like little soldier boy there. He's twigged. He knows me. Or is he guessing? I start to bring my legs together. Get ready.

I'll have to nail him quick. Get him in the throat.

Young man, flares Ellen, rising suddenly and stabbing at him with her finger, we are not girls. We do not want drinks. We do not want you or your attention. We want you to leave this table immediately.

I'm surprised. This is new to me. Baby Face winces. This is new to him, too. Women fighting back? Gwen gets up, starts yelling. Then Yvonne joins in. It's great. I'm cheering her on. Baby Face is reeling from the high-decibel verbal assault. Gwen picks up his fifty, throws it at him. The yelling gets louder. The barman rushes up. Baby Face is flushed, shouts, You fucking bitches. The barman grabs him, trundles him yelling out the door. I see his dark mate slip out the other door. I'm dazed.

Calm. Or relative peace. The three women mutter viciously, apologize to me. They hate being hustled in bars, have become very good at embarrassing the men who come on to them. I wonder if Baby Face is really the ex-MP from Vietnam. Has he made me, can he make the connection? I'm getting worried. We decide to leave. The lunch is in ruins emotionally. The women are angry about that, too.

Why can't we be left in peace, Yvonne cries.

We go out into the light, into the street; Yvonne's van has been trashed. Guess who. A steel bar or something. Busted windows and dents. The three of them decide they're going to the police. I beg off. I have a feeling that things are coming to a head. Involvement leads to questions. Questions lead to enquiries, computers. I might be all right if I play dumb. What does Baby Face know, anyhow? It doesn't matter. He's the one link I'm worried about. He's going to try to bargain his way out of his problem. Probably make up some bullshit. Enough to have them call me in, questions, papers I don't have, a search I don't want of the cabin. A fluke hookup with Australia. My sudden reappearance as an AWOL soldier. If I am. Maybe they've closed it down. Lost me in the file somewhere in Canberra. But I still don't know who those men were by the river, why they were killed. I've pinched the money, but it's the documents Wacker burned they probably want. It's a mess. I spin the coin in the car on the way home. Heads I stay, tails I go. Tails.

I pull out the three passports from Hong Kong. Canadian, American, Australian. The Canadian one is best. I tell the cockatiel to pack. I'm taking him home. Where? The cockatiel stops munching and stares at me.

You always wanted to go home. I say, C'mon I'm taking you. Aussie. Sunburnt plains and all that shit. Alice Springs. The sun. The red sand. Heat.

But how? I'm not sure . . . The cockatiel is strangely lost for words. Australia? Now?

You just hide inside my jacket, I say, and keep your trap shut and we'll just walk right on in, I say. You're smart enough for that. Do I have a choice? asks the cockatiel, pondering a rather large sunflower seed.

Nope. It's move or starve time, old mate.

Then, says the cockatiel, I shall pack immediately.

I'm about to leave a note for Yvonne when I hear the blat, blat of her VW van. She rushes in the door, sees my bag.

You're not leaving? She's shocked.

Yeah, I say quietly. There's a lot I have to tell you.

She comes closer. Little tears swim in her eyes.

That man. The big one, she says. The RCMP picked him up immediately. He was drunk and raving. An American. Up here fishing.

Yeah, I say, last time I saw him he was herring fishing. God knows who he really is.

Well, sighs Yvonne, he says he knows you. From Vietnam. The RCMP don't believe him. He's still drunk. He does know you, though, doesn't he?

Yeah. Unfinished business, love. There's a lot I have to tell you, but I want you to come with me.

I blew it there. I hadn't meant to say that. It just came out. I shouldn't get her involved.

Where?

Australia. I've got a lot of loose ends to clear up. Some money to give back. A few of my knuckles to get rapped. Nothing too big. Get your passport. We're off right now.

Australia? What about my job? My apartment? I can't just leave. Australia! Be serious, O'Donnell.

I shrug my shoulders. Just get sick, I say, give notice. Leave your landlord some money.

I show her the money belt, spread maybe five thousand U.S. dollars in front of her wide blue eyes.

She shakes her head. She grins that wide smile.

So I'm hooked up with a thief?

Not really. I'm a runaway.

I tell her the story. Briefly. Edited a bit. She listens intently. I finish.

She sits down. Silence for a while. Thinks. I stop packing. I get the feeling she's working things out.

I need your help, I say. She doesn't reply.

Look, she says finally. There's nothing for you to get so het up about. No one can prove anything. It's too long ago.

God. She has a lawyer's mind.

I wouldn't tell the Australian journalist anything, she adds, the press'd twist things about and blame you. Make you look compromised somehow.

No, Gerry's a good bloke, I protest.

It's not him, she says, they'd all be on to you like a pack of wolves.

What about Baby Face? I ask.

Oh, he's just another pawn in the game, she says.

Besides, she continues, the RCMP can't be bothered with what a drunk car smasher says. They've heard it all. The worst that can happen is that Immigration gets hold of you. That takes months. I'll call my brother. He can find out about you and the army. You've got to know sometime. And if things are not too desperate I'll take two weeks off starting next week. If you like, we can fly down to Australia then.

Christ, it's Wednesday. I'm still panicky. Four days.

I finger the penny. Damn it, that's my problem. I'm obsessed with luck. I don't think things through. Paranoid. Still crazy about shadows. Still think it's a movie I'm in.

I have to trust someone, sometime. And Yvonne is real.

Yvonne sits there. She is very beautiful. I think for a bit. The sea swings in slowly on a southeast swell. She's probably right. What the hell.

I get up, walk to her, take her in my arms.

You're on, I say, let's do it.

I can help you, she whispers in my ear.

She's right. But can I help her?

54

Perfectemente barracho, hiccups the cockatiel slumped at seven A.M. in all the bird seed and droppings at the bottom of its cage. A burp rolls like a slow whip up its body to crack softly the crested head. I look around. There's the sample bottle of tequila tipped on its side by the lectern.

You're really pissed. An all-night drunk? I say.

Yvonne, murmers the cockatiel, ignoring me. Why did you leave me?

One claw shakes frenetically.

Yvonne? I ask. *No se puede vivir sin amor,* it mumbles. I am one of those who have nobody them with.

Take it easy, I say soothingly.

Clear up your garden, asshole, cries the cockatiel. Fie on it, for 'tis rank and unweeded. Yvonne, Yvonne, moans the bird, *no se puede vivir sin amor.*

Sleep it off, I say, and pull the cage cover over the twitching feathers.

55

SHE TALKS TO HER BROTHER in Toronto for the longest time. Half an hour or more, maybe. She comes back to the sofa, looks at me and puts her arms around my neck. She looks into my eyes. I'm almost uncomfortable. It's almost too close.

He's going to make a couple of phone calls.

Now, wait, I begin to protest.

She puts her finger on my lips.

He'll be cautious, she continues, but like I said, it's probably all over. It's a dead issue. No one wants to hear about Vietnam any more. It wouldn't matter what you saw or did, it'd be just old news. The world's turned. David agrees.

Well, what's he phoning about?

She smiles. All confidence. I'm quaking. This could open up a big ants' nest.

Just to see if there's any warrants out for you, to see if anybody knows you're around, she says. You did give me your right name?

Of course, I protest. I wouldn't lie to her.

Well, Irish John O'Donnell, she smooths the part in my hair very slowly, descendant of Irish convicts, warrior, dashing wanderer of the world, gambler and roué, we'll find out if anybody knows anything about you. Oh, David wants to meet you. He says you sound intriguing.

What did you say? I ask, a little afraid.

He can meet you one of these days, she says, if he's lucky. He also says that idiot American who smashed my car'll be deported. He's checking on him, too.

How can he do all this? I marvel. In some strange way I'm pissed off, resentful. These people can pull strings, open doors, manipulate, while the poor sods at the other end get the shaft. It's like Adelaide again. Born south of the Torrens River and you're a struggler. Born north and you've got the easy ride. And the Torrens is a phony river too, plugged up artificially. It's true what Wacker used to say. Pick the wrong parents and pay for it for the rest of your life. It's not fair, but shit, what is. I need the help.

David, she says pensively, has spent his life getting to know the right people. He's very good at it.

Yeah, I add, well, I'm not exactly the right people. You dipped out there, love.

Yes, she says impishly, but with a bit of training you'll do very nicely.

I look out the window. The rain last night has washed away a lot of the snow. You can see patches of green grass, and in the little garden plot a tiny bud of purple, a crocus, the first sign of spring.

The phone rings. Yvonne goes to answer it. She talks for a while.

Outside the wind is southeast. Whitecaps run on the grey waves. A shower of rain splatters on the window as a gust takes it. Yvonne tells me the daffodils are next. I've never seen one growing. Hate the bloody things from that stupid poem at school about a host of yellow freaks dancing. Christ, when we studied that it was about 110 degrees Fahrenheit, and the whole earth at Woodville High was baked dead flat and dry. There wasn't even enough water pressure in the drinking taps to squirt the other kids. Poms. They'd taken Australia to the cleaners for years. I remember how pissed off my dad was when Don Bradman became Sir Donald Bradman after years of belting the Pommy bowlers all over the shop. But it hadn't been them who'd sucked us into Vietnam. It was the Yanks. Probably the bloody CIA and God knows what other threats.

Yvonne hangs up and dances back, skips onto the sofa and gives me a huge hug and kiss.

Oh boy, she cries, this is the first time I've kissed someone who's officially dead.

What? I'm stunned.

Yes, she laughs. David thinks it's a huge joke. He got the RCMP to telex Australia. John O'Donnell is missing in action in Vietnam. Isn't that just too weird? And the American's an ex-Marine, a drifter, a petty thief from L.A. He'll be deported for sure.

Byzantine, I begin to say, but change my mind. So they did stuff it up. The paper did get shuffled sideways and arsed about and some rear-end clerk just solved it with a quick stamp. I feel tremendously relieved. Until I think about it. If Jack O'Donnell's dead, then who the fuck am I? The bits have all fallen neatly into a lucky break, but it raises other problems I'm not sure about.

Yeah, but how do I get around that? I ask Yvonne, puzzled. Like, who do I become now?

Anybody, Yvonne shrieks, you've been born again. You can be anybody you want.

It's too much for me to take in. I get up and walk to the window. The rain's pelting down now. You can see little holes in what's left of the snow. Yvonne comes up and grabs me around the waist.

What's the matter, she asks huskily.

I dunno, I say, I don't know where to begin now. What to do.

Ah, Jackie boy, she says in mock Irish, it's you that's come out of the grave and has the whole world as your oyster now. You're free Jack. Don't you understand? You're free.

I want to smuggle that damn bird in and let it go in the desert, I say suddenly.

The bird? She's very surprised. Why the bird?

Oh, I dunno. It's wrong for it to be in a cage here. It should be free, too.

A bird in a cage sets Heaven in a rage, Blake says.

I can't tell her the whole truth, damn it. She'll think the cockatiel's voice is all in my mind. I know for sure it's real.

That could be difficult, she says, smuggling it in.

Nah, I say confidently. We'll dope the little bastard. Let it sleep in my inside pocket. They'll never catch on.

I don't know, O'Donnell, Yvonne says, puzzled, you just get out of one scrape and you're risking another.

Ah, the bird's no trouble.

I go to the telephone.

What are you doing, she asks.

Booking two flights return to Sydney and Alice Springs, Australia, I say confidently. For the first time in a long while I feel like I'm in charge of my life.

56

GOD, SIGHS THE COCKATIEL, it's hard not to be disgusted by the violence and cruelty you portray. The bird is reading my notebooks. I had them all out ready to pack. Take this horrible wiring up of flesh you describe. The bird taps at a sheet of my writing. Or this, the bird shuffles and hops to the description of the two murdered Yanks. Obscene! Absolutely obscene! cries the bird, shaking its head in dismay. And yet you claim to be civilized, to have culture, a developed perception.

We are, I respond. War is just an aberration. Put it up against all the diverse and complex machines, the intricacies of cities, architecture, art, music, literature, government, sports, our social customs . . . I run out there. Man's achievement does seem pretty extensive, though the bird cackles in horrific mirth. It waddles over to face me, and its hackles rise, its beak snaps.

Primitive pigs, the bird snarls, mired in atavistic ritual, in primitive superstition.

Come on, I cry, we're the bosses, rulers of the earth, we're sophisticated, higher intelligences. You're just sprouting sour bird seed.

This enrages the cockatiel. Let us look, the bird shrieks, at your social customs. Let us examine the apparent civilized core, the well-wrought fabric of your so-called society.

Take for example your marriage, or better, your wedding. The most primitive of rituals. The bride is dressed in fancy white. Now this white which is supposed to have a symbolic significance is often a tremendous lie. Where are the virgins, tell me that! And attending her, for no logical reason, are two or three other women, not dressed in white. Does this mean they are sluts and cannot wear white? What is their function? To restrain a lustful bridegroom until the strange ceremony is over? To ensure the bride doesn't run off? And why, tell me, does the bride carry something old, something new, something borrowed and something blue?

I dunno, I say, it's just tradition.

Tradition! screams the bird. Like war, I suppose. No, it's mindless tribal superstition! exclaims the bird. And her horseshoes, the bird continues, are mere atavism. Worse, her father throws her away, glad no doubt, to get rid of the silly woman. Not to mention the flowers all the females carry, an open and blatant symbol of their attempt at sexual attention, flaunting their openness, like the coloured flowers to the bee, their availability for conception.

That's a bit thick, I mumble.

Oh, there's more, says the bird, prancing now with indignation. Tell me why the witch doctor chants at the front of this tribal gathering, he too, dressed in strange and abnormal garb. And why does the tribe jump up and yell and sit down, and kneel and mumble at his command? Have they no minds of their own? And the round chunk of metal twisted painfully onto the bride's finger, to stay forever, a kind of branding, or possession, and the bunch of flowers the bride throws up so a group of other young women can fight and scratch and grab for their chance at the same bizarre experience? Oh yes, quite civilized, quite logical, the bird says scathingly. And the tin cans and signs and abuse tied to the getaway vehicle? Why do they have to escape? Will the ritual turn into violence? Very logical. Not to mention the dangerous and wasteful throwing of food at the couple as they run the gauntlet after the ceremony, as if the whole tribe has turned on them and wants to be rid of them.

Okay, I say, weddings are a bit different.

Oh, cries the cockatiel, full of righteous wrath, what about a rabbit that lays eggs at Easter time; chocolate ones, too! Biologically very sound, eh? Or a night when innocent children are dressed as witches, goblins, werewolves and vampires and sent out as hoodlums, to terrify the neighbourhood, to establish a protection racket to avoid them wreaking havoc on the whole community?

Ah, that's just kids' stuff, I say. Halloween is fun.

Fun, shrieks the cockatiel, it's crazy. It's mumbo jumbo tribal nonsense. Not to mention the old fat man dressed in red with his ho ho ho who lies deliberately to all the children about his miraculous ability. In the space of a few hours, he will climb down chimneys and produce all kinds of toys for them. It's a perpetuated deliberate falsehood foisted on millions of innocents every year. Add to that the extended slaughter of all kinds of birds and trees, and the piggish drinking and eating that goes on for days, and the illicit kissing under foliage and the tribal drunkenness of New Year's. And the tooth fairy who exchanges silver for rotten cuspids. Oh, no. Totally primitive. Even your team sports, so touted, ones that I notice you watch endlessly on that idiot box over there, are merely symbolic wars, wars of the colours, better than the real ones, but still very stupid, like the red and green factions of ancient Rome. They fight and bash and tear away at each other for the possession of one simple silly object, a puck, or a ball, to be taken from one end of a stadium to another. Quite absurd. Totally tribal. I must say the stripes and slashes and drawings on their helmets and uniforms are quite childish. There's one particularly garish lot, completely tasteless, in black and red and yellow.

The Canucks? I offer.

Yes, that's the tribe. Wouldn't they all be happy if they were given a ball each?

That's not the point, I say, it's a game.

It is, the bird cries, a tribal ritual. Ah, my heart bleeds (here, the cockatiel crosses its heart with its right claw) for the innocent young, so absurdly brought up as humans, their notion of identity, sexuality and courtship, and success so mired, so deeply stuck in the primeval ooze of human ritual. And all this perpetuated visually in colour on that idiot image box you are so enamoured of. You can hardly take your eyes off it.

It's not so bad, I say, defensively. For the bird has made a point or two, I must admit.

Bad, shrieks the bird. Consider the small child, held in the arms of an outrageously garbed witch doctor, in front of his parents and the whole tribe, who is assaulted, not once but thrice with cold water, thrown on his bare head. Or worse, in some strange and even more primitive religious subgroups, the poor thing is actually nearly drowned three times so it can be admitted to the tribe. Shockingly primitive. Or that other religious subgroup who insist on feeding the kneeling tribe with magic bread and magic booze. Isn't that tragic and misinformed? Shall I go on?

No, I say, you've made your point. I'm going for a walk.

What about the horror and violence in children's fairy tales? Disembowelled animals and decapitation. Little Miss Bloody Red Riding Hood. What about the red poppies? What about the brutality of circumcision? the bird shrieks at my departing back.

The bird is right. I had been involved in a weird and illogical tribal killing game. It amounted to nothing. We performed the ritual, followed the rules. Nothing changed. We're all back home or dead. They've got the rice paddies. It was a stupid dramatic performance. A bloody play. It is as if nothing changed. Except the agony and blood of young men. It's depressing. Enough to bring tears to a glass eye. I walk onto the beach. Above, a thin V-shape of geese moves slowly north. At least they have the sense to migrate. Nations mean nothing to them, should mean nothing to me. A man's a damn sight better off without a nation. All you end up doing is killing and dying over a stupid flag. For a team. For a stupid bloody game played by men in dress-up clothes. It was insane.

57

THERE WAS ONE LETTER I KEPT. Wacker tossed them all in a heap in the rubbish bin out the back of the tent, and burned them. But not this one. I've carried it with me now in that thin money belt ever since. I don't even have to get it out to remember what it says. At first I kept it as a souvenir. A kind of ironic comment on the pointlessness of all the poor sods around me getting mangled and bloodied in the jungle while the banana-brained peaceniks marched against the war back home. We used to get angry and confused and frustrated about that. At first we wanted to get the whole RAR back home, lined up on North Terrace on full automatic when the beards-and-beads bastards came tromping down from the Uni, and just let fly. Then, week by week, someone's sister'd write and say she was going on the march, to try to get us home safe, and someone's mother and even Harris's grandpa, who'd been in Tobruk, wrote and said he was going on the next march, because the Yanks'd sucked Australia into a crook war. So in the end we just dropped it, forgot it, gave it a miss, decided it was out of whack. We went on patrol and just tried to last the distance, to stay alive.

I thought this letter was just another white-arse liberal effort at getting out of the war or out of the U.S. draft. It took me a long time to realize it was different, that I was sitting on dynamite.

I remember without looking, it had an emblem, a seal of some kind, on the letterhead, an eagle I think, or some kind of official U.S. embossing standing out on the paper. I know now how ironic that eagle symbol is. They're damn near extinct in the

States, though lots of them fly about freely here. It was addressed to the Provisional Government of the People's Socialist Republic of Vietnam, which didn't exist as far as I knew. There was a whole lot I didn't know. But this is what the letter said.

> The members of the United States Nation-at-Large whose signatures appear on the closure of this document hereby state their political opposition to the U.S. armed intervention in the internal affairs of Vietnam.
>
> Furthermore, the undersigned are willing to undertake confidential negotiations to bring an end to hostilities in order to bring about the official repatriation of U.S. troops currently in Vietnam. These negotiations could take place under the auspices of a neutral government to be so named by the representatives of the People's Socialist Republic of Vietnam.
>
> It should be stressed that the confidentiality of any such unofficial talks is crucial and the bearers of this document are empowered by the undersigned to establish a preliminary context for negotiations.

And then the letter is signed by a couple of senators, half a dozen congressmen, two movie stars I recognized and a bunch of other Yanks whose names didn't ring a bell at all. Fifteen signatures in all. Of course, they didn't mention the Aussie or the Kiwi troops who were out there getting shot at for no good reason either. We didn't count. I remember reading about Fulbright, the U.S. senator, coming down to Australia once and being surprised when he was told there were Australian troops in Vietnam. He didn't know, though he should have, because he was the chairman of some senate committee involved in the whole damn war. That upset us a lot.

I find this hard to believe, says the cockatiel, alighting on my shoulder and quickly scanning the letter, though one of those senators is a flake from a well known and bizarre liberal family. But I can hardly imagine all these celebrities risking their reputations and wealth on such a will-o'-the-wisp endeavour. Why, they could easily be arrested as traitors. No, the document must be a very clever forgery. Most impressive deceit, I must say. The cockatiel nods wisely.

They could just be sincere concerned citizens, willing to take a chance to stop the war, I offer.

My dear boy, chuckles the cockatiel, you are so naive politically. Even after what you've been through. No. Human nature is, I believe, as Machiavelli puts it, tuned to the grossest of self-interest. No. It's more likely some devious persons forged this letter to embarrass the names included at the bottom—to discredit them and their efforts to end the war. Don't you see how effective that would be? The poor chaps'd be so busy denying their part in this letter that their usefulness as an antiwar force would be spent. A delicate, if Byzantine manoeuvre, I must say.

Christ, I think, the cockatiel is using Wacker's word.

I don't think so, I say, those two kids were killed because they had this letter and some other powerful bastards wanted it.

Pouf, says the bird, they were, as that dreadful nasal pop singer states, mere pawns in the game. Totally expendable. Their deaths merely added credibility to the seriousness of the charges that could be laid against the signatories—traitors, and by implication, accessories to murder.

Now the bird has me thinking. What if it's right? Who am I protecting by keeping this letter?

Of course, cries the bird, I'd have to examine the signatures to be certain, but I've no doubt it's a very clever FBI or CIA plant. The only thing that went wrong is that they hadn't counted on your kleptomania. They were hoping for some noble and honest chevalier to find it and reveal it to the world.

Double Barrel, I think instantly, the perfect fit. He'd tell everybody. It's his breeding. He was so true blue it hurt. He'd be perfect for them.

And think, chortles the cockatiel, of the exquisite strait jacket they've put you in.

What do you mean? I ask.

Well, you can say absolutely nothing now, giggles the cockatiel. Oh, I just love it. You won't dare make the letter public because they'll charge you with murder of those two young Americans. It's quintessentially Machiavellian. The end justifies the means. And what clever means.

They couldn't, I say; all the others were there. They saw the two Yanks. Dead on the ground.

Yes, smiles the cockatiel, but where are your comrades all

now? Pushing up daisies. There's just your word against whoever they wish to produce to prove you're a desperate thief, liar, and murderer. I expect it's an open-and-shut case.

I'm stunned. The cockatiel is right. Wacker, Double Barrel, Harris, the lot. They're all gone. It would be my word against theirs, and little hope for the poor bloke from Down Under.

The cockatiel flies off to the reading lectern, turns a page, and begins reading again. I walk over to the stand. Sure enough, the book the bird is reading is Machiavelli's *The Prince.*

Well, that bird's little speech has me really stuffed. Screwed, blued, and tattooed. If he is right I can't blow open the story anywhere, even if there were a bit of passing interest. It'd backfire on me. My best bet is to turn up in Adelaide and claim I had a bit of a breakdown towards the end. Or else I could just go on living, knowing that old O'Donnell is dead and that I've been miraculously and fortuitously reborn, returned unofficially to the earth to begin a new life.

As Yvonne's brother said, I am old news. No one wants to know about it anyhow. Baby Face, whatever his part in the whole business, was a nobody like me, puffed up to importance by the hothouse of war. They'd deny his assertions whatever they are. He would be an embarrassment to the Yanks. They'd want to find a large carpet and sweep Baby Face and whatever he knew or did right under with all the other bits of history no one wants to know. Probably quite forcefully. If I keep my mouth shut, I'm okay. If I don't, someone might want to shut it for me. Everybody wants to forget the shambles of Vietnam. It's about time I did, too. Clear the slate. Put up the numbers for the next race. Get on with living.

I take the letter, open the woodstove, shove the sheet of paper inside, and light it with a match. A bright yellow flame flares up, consumes whatever truth it contained. Ashes to ashes. Purging by fire. I think of a napalm strike we reconnoitred a day after the Yank jets had let fly. Four bodies lay crumpled, black and crisped up like the remnants of the letter in the fire. No one could tell if they were friend or foe.

58

WE LAND IN ALICE at about three in the afternoon. The sand shimmers like red molten glass. We've been flying now for about twenty hours. We're pretty well jet-lagged into exhaustion. The cockatiel sleeps inside my Hong Kong jacket. It's been asleep for hours. Yvonne leans her head on my shoulder. She's just fallen asleep. After the first hundred miles of red sand and dark red ridges she lost interest in the Centre. It's not just red though. It's every kind of tan and gold and pink as well. She's missing the shimmering salt flats and the tiny flash of homesteads every now and then, the iron roofs in the sun and the little splash of drab green trees about the water the sheds nestle into. I'm fascinated. It has a richness I'd forgotten, this place, a tough but beautiful variety to it.

We drive in a taxi through The Gap. The town has grown, spread out. We pass green ovals and houses with flower gardens. I think it's too civilized, but Yvonne is enchanted. That's the difference between us. Black kids everywhere. We stop at the Alice Springs Hotel. Two black men in dirty singlets and baggy trousers move in on us, crowding us, demanding money. I start to push them back a bit, but Yvonne scrambles in her purse, gives them some coins. Cheap bitch, one of them yells at her back as we go through the glass doors of the hotel. I just shake my head. She can handle that stuff much better than I can.

I leave them there in the room and walk down to the Elders building, trying to get there just before five. Wacker's brother Peter should get off work then and I want to have a beer with him, explain things, hand back the penny, slip him a few dollars, tell him about Wacker, get some of this stuff off my back.

His secretary shows me in reluctantly. Peter stands up. At twenty-five he's already got a beer gut over the tailored shorts, white shirt and tie. He's polite but not really pleased to see me. Too many memories. I've heard of this situation before. They're angry that you're alive and their brother or son isn't. I make it brief. He listens, gets up, walks to the window. He was alive when you saw him last? he asks.

Wounded, but alive, yeah. But there's not much chance, I trailed off.

You left him? The question is flat, objective.

I had no choice, mate. He couldn't walk. I didn't tell him about the craziness, the threat to shoot me if I didn't run, the bloody pulp of his feet. What was the point.

I produce the penny, put it on his desk. He gave me this. Before I left.

He picks it up, gives it back. I don't want the bloody thing, he says, it killed Grandpa, then the Old Man, and now Wacker. It's Australian bullshit. That's not luck in that thing. It's something worse.

I get up, pocket the penny. No point in staying here. He's seen enough of me. I mention a quick beer but he declines, leans heavily forward on his desk, his head down.

I'm sorry, I say. Though what for, I'm not sure. For being alive? To hell with that! I leave. He's still standing there leaning forward on his desk as if deep in some thought. Maybe he's remembering Wacker playing cricket or drinking beer or spinning a yarn, one of those quick little movies we have of the dead, animated and colourful and so very sad.

Back at the hotel the cockatiel nods on the bedstead. Fast asleep, Yvonne lies across the bed. I pick up her legs, straighten her up, fall asleep myself.

Next morning I bring the rented Landcruiser back to the front of the hotel. Yvonne is breezy and refreshed. The cockatiel peeks out from inside her jacket. It's surprisingly quiet. Hasn't said a word for ages.

We drive twenty miles north and then off the highway into the sand due west for an hour. The heat begins to shimmer in the distance. Already I'm beginning to miss the mountains and water and soft clouds of Vancouver Island. We drive down a dry creek bed and Yvonne discovers some Sturt peas, little red and dark blue buds here in this blood sand. The cockatiel screeches unintelligibly. It strikes me that the bloody bird hasn't said a word since we got on the plane in Vancouver.

What's wrong with you? I ask it.

Its beak opens and a high repeated shriek is all that comes out. It's excited, Yvonne says. Where are you going to let it free?

I look ahead. There's a little clump, almost a ring of scrub. Probably a tiny water hole. We drive towards it, stop. A flight of parrots busts from the scrub, wheels like a streamer and zings off to the west.

I hold the cockatiel high in my hand. Go on, I cry, Fuck off! It's what you want, isn't it? Do it!

The cockatiel flexes its wings, beats briefly, and then with a cry, leaps from my fingers and flies with its burst and dip and burst and dip farther and farther, past the water hole, farther to the west until I can see it no longer. Yvonne stands looking at where the bird disappeared.

I finger the penny in my pocket, bring it out, spin it several times in the bright sunlight. I look at Yvonne again. Again the similarity hits me. She could be Wacker's sister. No dead ringer mind you, but something about her, the wide grin, the ability to get along, the courage, the inner spirit.

I toss the penny high and wide behind my back. Suddenly I feel so light, as if I've got wings, as if I could fly. I turn to her. She smiles, grabs me.

What are you thinking, O'Donnell? she asks.

I think I'm ready for you now, I say.

Yeah, but am I ready for you? she replies.

It's a fair question.

Gary Peters

Kevin Roberts was born in Adelaide, Australia, where he attended university; after that he worked as a roustabout on sheep stations and wheat farms. In 1965 he sailed to Canada, where he taught high school in Dawson Creek before attending graduate school at Simon Fraser University near Vancouver. For a number of years he followed his passion for fishing and boats by running his own troller. Since 1969 he has taught English at Malaspina College in Nanaimo, B.C. He lives on the beach in Lantzville on Vancouver Island with his family.

Kevin Roberts has published two collections of short fiction, one play and seven volumes of poetry. His poems and fiction have also appeared in many literary magazines and been selected for a number of anthologies.

DOUGLAS & McINTYRE FICTION

SERIES EDITOR: RON SMITH

Fire Eyes by D. F. Bailey

From the Belly of a Flying Whale by Byrna Barclay

Zero Avenue by Leona Gom

The Saxophone Winter by Robert Harlow

The Watery Part of the World by Gladys Hindmarch

Crossings by Betty Lambert

Hear Us O Lord from Heaven Thy Dwelling Place by Malcolm Lowry

October Ferry to Gabriola by Malcolm Lowry

The True Story of Ida Johnson by Sharon Riis

North of the Battle by Merna Summers